Her Blanket of Stars.

ORLA
KELLY
PUBLISHING

Maryjka Miller

And I'd choose you,
in a hundred lifetimes,
in a hundred worlds,
in any version of reality,
I'd find you
and I'd choose you.

Kiersten White

Thank you to my partner Stu for all your love and support.

With you by my side, I feel there's nothing I cannot do. You are, without doubt, the best thing that has ever happened to me and home is where you and Molly are.

You are, always have been and always will be my North Star.

Acknowledgements

Mum and Dad, thank you for your unwavering support, not just during the writing of this book but throughout every chapter of my life. You have always allowed me to colour outside the lines and to dance to my own drumbeat! You have always been my greatest champions! I smile when I think of your beautiful love story; this is where the romantic in me was born!

Lynny, my only sister but the equivalent of ten! I admire you so much for the daughter, sister and mother that you are. You are way beyond kind, caring, thoughtful, loving and generous. I'm so unbelievably grateful to have you in my life.

David, you have always had a talent for making me feel special, loved and accepted. You have always inspired me and I treasure our time together. You are never more than a thought away. Where I go you go.

Kev, you are my younger brother, but I continue to look up to you! I admire the way that you live your life with such authenticity, strength, positivity, resilience and kindness towards those around you. I know you always have my back and I have yours.

Meg, Chloe, Jamie, Lucy, Harry, Saoirse, Charlie, Fionn and Oisin…my precious nieces and nephews, you are the sunflowers in my garden, the sprinkles on my sundae and the beat in my heart.

Thank you to my publisher Orla Kelly, for all your guidance and professionalism.

Over the past year, while working on this book, I have been gifted with the support, kindness, and encouragement of a number of family members and friends. Although too numerous to mention, I trust you know who you are and to you all, I extend my deepest gratitude. I extend special thanks to Leen & Frank, Erica & Alison, San, Rach, Judy, Phil, Mary, Lawrence, Jacqui, Helena, Damien, Thomas and Terry. A final special mention to John & Mar, Uncle Tadhg, Uncle Kev, my beautiful Grandmother Gretta and my much-loved Godfather, Pat.

Contents

Contents Cont.

1

Come forth the actress for there is no other role to play

She closed the red door behind her, anxious to set off on the short journey for her first day at her new music course. She took a few steps and stopped dead in her tracks and looked back at the door behind her.

Did I lock it? I did, but then it's such an automatic response maybe I didn't.

She had to put her mind at rest, otherwise she would spend the day distracted, so she walked back to the door and pulled down the handle to check. It was locked. She checked it two more times, slowly raising the handle up and down, like some sort of uninvited, weird ritual. Satisfied, she continued on her way. She scolded herself for doubting her original intuition, and as she walked, she glanced to her right, soaking up the view of the city that presented itself across the rooftops. At that moment, she noticed for the millionth time, how dirty Cork city looked and how she would love to get a giant power washer and clean it, together with all the other buildings. In a perfect world that would somehow wash away any of its impurities. Everything could then get a fresh lick of paint and flowers could decorate the scenery. She soon realised she was fantasising again and wasting precious time thinking pie-in-the-sky ideas. It might have been a dirty city, but it was her city, and she loved it anyway, in a love/hate kind of way.

See the good! The air felt fresh on her face and in her lungs and with birds landing on rooftops and dogs barking nearby, there was a comfortable familiarity. Nature always had a way of calming her. She then remembered to keep her eyes down. Her neighbourhood was a pit-stop for drug users, and every so often she would find used heroin needles hanging around. It was routine for her to scan the ground every day she left her house, and once she left the neighbourhood she felt she could look up once again and enjoy her surroundings.

'Hey Blondie,' jeered the resident drug user, while sitting hunched over on the steps close to the exit of the neighbourhood.

'Oh, hi,' muttered Georgia, careful not to sound too friendly. She didn't want to appear too approachable as she felt that would only encourage him, but she also knew that if she ignored him that would draw him closer. She had only watched him inject heroin into his girlfriend on the same grubby steps a couple of days previous. She shuddered inside at the memory and kept her stride, heading down more steep steps to enter the main street.

'Blondie?! you absolute dick. What is my life right now?' she mumbled under her breath when he was out of earshot.

Focus, there will always be annoyances. You are on a mission. Come on, happy thoughts. She quickly walked up the hill to the new building. It was only ten minutes away, and it was right across the road from where she had gone to secondary school as a young girl. She was thinking to herself, thank God it's so near as she was certainly not a morning person. This course was not taking place in a University but more of a community music college. Her long elbow-length, thick, blonde, wavy hair was tied up in a neat ballerina bun with not a hair out of place. It had taken her an hour to style earlier that morning, and she could feel her head ache with the tightness of the bun. She wore light make up as she reckoned the natural look did her more justice.

After much reflection on what to wear, she had settled on the petrol blue tunic, knee-length cotton dress over black leggings and knee-high, wine faux leather boots to complete the look. She wore a navy, waist-length pea coat to keep her warm as this was February in Ireland and it was cold, very cold. She didn't want to look like she was trying too hard but instead look like she belonged in the music scene. This look had to be cool but subtle. Appearance was everything, even though she was literally dying of nerves she could not let that be seen. She felt like her stomach had its own pulse, and her palms were getting more and more sweaty by the minute. She was noticing now, how she had rubbed her neck numerous times on her journey and how her hands seemed to be in overdrive. Nevertheless, in her mind she had to look in control, calm, confident, charming, friendly and open. She had it all planned out, and she was just going to have to act her way through it, and not show these strangers her real self as that would just make her feel vulnerable. No, she had to stay in control. It's how she approached everything in life. Don't let the guard down or you'll get stamped on. Life had taught her this lesson and it was a cruel lesson but one she would learn from and take to heart fully.

When she arrived at the gates of her old school, she cast her eyes to the left to breathe in her old secondary school momentarily. She hadn't frequented this side of the city in many years, and she wanted to see her old school in a positive light but instead felt discomfort at the reminder of an unhappy time in her life. It had been roughly fourteen years since she had come by this way, and she never expected to frequent it again, but life is funny. For one reason or another, it can take you down roads that you promised to never walk again. She took a deep breath, straightened herself, put her game face on and took her final short hill to the music course across the road on the right. It was a massive, old, red brick school building called the Abbey Music Community College. She saw a door to the left side and entered in walking tall and straight as if she had been going there for years, and noticed a man in the doorway.

Great, I can ask him for directions to the office. God, this is nerve-racking, she mused. It seemed like a hive of activity with students, young and old, making their way to their different classrooms. This somewhat friendly-looking chap of stocky build and sporting red hair pointed her to the office. She was then directed upstairs where she found her new class. The class had not yet started, so she had time to scan the room. There were rows of tables and chairs down the middle and on either side, and she decided to pick the empty seat in the middle of the classroom.

Yes, this felt comfortable, not too close to the top, not off to one side. She felt she could use this spot to observe people and feel at a comfortable distance from her teacher.

Her music teacher arrived in. He was over 6ft tall, slim with black hair, nice looking, with a truly kind face and gentle smile. She assumed he was in his early forties. He wore a casual baby blue sweater teamed with black trousers, and she instantly liked his vibe. This was especially important as she had loathed her previous teacher. Before this, she had been studying Japanese at University level, but she was forced to quit. This she did with a heavy heart as she had excelled at learning the language, but her lecturer, Shiko, had been a bully. She was a middle-aged Japanese lady who had missed her calling as an Army drill sergeant and had the tolerance of a lightning storm. Georgia had been the only student in her class. Her fellow college classmates had all picked Chinese or Korean as they had heard on the grapevine that Japanese was too difficult. Georgia had been reciting it in essays, having conversations in Japanese, and learnt two particles of the language in just a weekend. Her teacher had often accused her of having studied Japanese before and was relentless with pressure tactics for her to learn more. She wanted her to try harder, even though she had been studying every spare hour and was literally in tears at the way the course was going. No, this music course was her fresh start. Her chance to change direction and get it right once and for all, so the teacher was a vital component to get right.

Box ticked, she reflected, as she glimpsed at her new classmates whose ages seemed to vary from approximately twenty to sixty years of age. *Interesting, A good mix in ages would make for an intriguing dynamic,* so this pleased her.

It was mostly men in her class, of which she had now counted as twenty people, four of which were female. Where this might be daunting to some girls, Georgia had found much solace in men. She was comfortable with them and felt safe in their company. *A little intimidating nonetheless, but this could work.* Class proceeded, and two hours later it was time for a tea break. Georgia was relieved as she was a smoker, an avid coffee drinker, and needed both substances to calm her nerves. When she saw that people were getting ready to go downstairs to a canteen she just followed their lead. She got herself a coffee from a nice, blonde, foreign canteen lady and asked an older guy where the smoking area was.

The canteen resembled a huge Community hall full of tables and chairs and a stage at the bottom of the room. It all looked so old school, but she had read that this was once a Catholic Boys School so she supposed it made sense, however strange. She was directed to the outside of the building from the canteen on the right. An old, bolted, steel door swung open, and there she noticed a group of men smoking. The area reminded her of an oversized bus shelter, and a heavy-set man with dark hair and a sheepish grin beckoned her over to join them for a cigarette. She smiled and joined them offering her name and a polite handshake. They seemed a bit aghast that this small 5ft 4", slim, cute, little blonde seemed unafraid to join them despite it being all men. They started to ask her questions and pleasantries to break the ice.

'What's your name? Did you just start today? I haven't seen you before,' they communicated.

The group of guys seemed to increase in numbers, and before long one became two and two became ten. Some guys formed little groups. Others had their foot against the wall. A couple of guys spread out looking like loners just wanting to enjoy their puff with a coffee in hand and in between all that crowd stood a man. A man who had noticed her the minute she came flying out those canteen doors.

Who the hell is she? What the heck? He felt like he had just been grabbed and shook. He felt a weird feeling in his stomach like it had flipped. There was an energy to this smoking area he had not felt before. It was a woman's energy and it wasn't just any woman; it was this force of nature. *Where in the world did she come from?* He sheepishly stood back from the crowd of men and took it upon himself to observe her. He wasn't ready to meet her, God no, but he was thrilled and excited that he could just drink her in. She was short and wearing this cool quirky baby doll dress and these funky knee-high boots. *The way she had walked out screamed confidence and self-assurance, but not cocky. Just the right amount of confidence.* He studied her body and noticed she had a curve to her waist like an hourglass shape. It was hard to fully analyse as her dress was loose. As he looked up higher he saw her medium size chest covered up to the neck.

Hmm, fully covered, that's classy and mysterious. He was used to seeing girls having plenty on show, but this intrigued him and then he looked at her face. He noticed her lightly tanned, soft, oval-shaped face and was struck by her eyes.

Jeez, what is behind those blue eyes? They are piercing. He had never seen eyes like hers before. *There was a story behind these, a million stories, and they were just so unreachable.*

Her lips were wide and full, and he watched with enthusiasm as she laughed a little through conversation with the guys. Little did he realise at the time that this force of nature would go on to haunt him for years. The damage was done. He was hooked and had to know more.

For starters, is she Swedish? Hmm, she looks like that with her pale, blonde hair, icy eyes and foreign Nordic-looking features. He would have to get closer to know more, but not today. This would have to be a slow burner because heck, she was intimidating.

Georgia's nerves began to ease a little after breaking the ice now with the guys. She had managed to keep her cool and return to class, ready for the next two hours before home time. She noticed that there was an adjoining classroom onto hers, and students had dribbled through at various stages, possibly going to the office with papers in hand.

Well, there's probably another twenty in that room, and then it looked like more classes were being run downstairs. Right, enough speculation for now. One o'clock speedily arrived and she bounced up from the table and quickly made her way down the stairs and breezed out the door eager to get home. *Woah, it had been an exhausting day, first damn day, always the hardest but it would get easier with every passing one. She would get used to it, and they would get used to her. She would befriend them all yet and charm her way around them. She had to, to make it work. She had to make this college feel like home so that she wouldn't end up doing what she had always done, up and leave.*

2

Show me the door, for I shall walk through it, and keep on walking, be it the road to nowhere

She had been doing that since secondary school. She was always coming up with reasons why it wasn't working and why she needed her freedom. She had always been a girl off the beaten track. As a child, she liked to go to school wearing a pink jumper over her brown school uniform with green socks, or sometimes no socks. Her schoolteacher mother would scold her, explaining that this clothing combination wasn't appropriate, but her mother just knew this child was strong-willed and would beat to her own drum. Georgia was very shy in school and never paid attention. Instead she would daydream or mess around with her school friends. The school reports all said the same thing. 'Georgia has great potential if she would just try harder.' Primary school went in a fuzz, and her same behaviour continued on into secondary school.

She would continue to repeat the same behaviours, but for some reason she proved popular and made friends with a lot of the girls in her all-girls school. She found herself a tight-knit group of buddies, but once again daydreamed her classes away, still managing to get good enough grades with no study. After a while, she was dropped down into the second-lowest ability class, with a mixture of nice girls, chavs, bullies, and of course the freaky types too. She took it all in her stride, but she had no confidence with her mousy brown hair, soft, size 14 body, and ordinary looks. She felt like an ugly duckling, and no boys showed any interest in her at any school discos or in any social setting. She longed to be seen by boys, as was typical of girls her age, and they did see her, but unfortunately not how she had hoped. She had overheard a boy saying at a school disco that he wouldn't touch her with a 50ft pole with a condom at the end of it. Other times she would hear guys snigger about her fat ass. She was either invisible or the butt of somebody's jokes. This naive, innocent girl with a heart of gold, who her mother would refer to as Cinderella, would just want to be nice to everyone. However, she was learning fast that maybe she needed to change tactic and become more assertive.

She began to spend many of her days skipping school and going into the city, just ten minutes away. These frequent trips into town, while she was meant to be in school, were where she found refuge from the frustration of school, and her hatred of it. It was where she would learn her first lesson in independence, and it empowered her. Most days she just had to escape, and when she went home, she escaped into TV land. Her younger brother, Oscar, would tease her on the fact that they didn't need a TV guide when they had Georgia. She would know every programme that was scheduled. Life was a blur with her just plodding along until things came to a head one day. A mean, chavvy girl bullying one of her friends in class resulted in Georgia standing her ground, shouting down the bully and storming out of the class. She thundered down the school stairs to her locker in a temper. She emptied her school locker into her school bag and stood still in a trance, looking at it as if she was having a brainstorm.

I'm gone, I won't even tell my friends. A rush of power ran through her, and she smiled with glee. This is the moment she had been waiting for. She had been wanting to leave since 1st year but just needed a good enough reason. She felt empowered, liberated, and sure. *Yes, she was only in 5th year at this stage and had no Leaving Cert but screw it, who cares? I'm free, I'll do what I want. Nobody is ever going to keep me down. I'm my own boss and God damn it, it's my life.* This ended up being the beginning of a repetitive theme in her life. The story of her life and the pattern that would just never die. Her mother agreed that she could leave school but only on condition that she picked a course or a job, so after careful consideration she picked a beauty course in the city centre.

By now she was seventeen and she started a beautician course in a private college, 6 miles from her family home in Blarney. She really liked her classmates and over that year she lost weight, learned how to style herself properly, do her makeup, highlight her attributes, and overhaul her walk, look and personality. This is when the ugly duckling became a swan. She now started to frequent nightclubs and suddenly men were stopping her all the time, telling her she was a knockout. Men would stare and smile and give her the star treatment. What had once been a famine was now the unbelievable opposite. Her hair was now highlighted blonde, and she began to understand if you want to be confident, you've got to act until it becomes real, so she put her shoulders back, lifted her head up high, and walked with purpose. 'Fake it until you make it,' her older classmate Kelly had advised her one afternoon in class, as they hooked each other up on the muscle toning machines. Georgia found herself hungry for more knowledge and started to read girly magazines to get the low down on everything. She kept practising her new mannerisms until she began to feel confident for real. She had seen a quote on a café window, 'Believing is half of being,' and that had got her thinking too.

She couldn't believe her plan had worked but even though this beautiful woman had emerged out of nowhere, she never forgot her roots or her days as the ugly duckling, and what that had felt like. The girl nobody noticed had hurt her deeply. Life had taught her to be nice to everyone, be kind, and never forget where you came from. That ugly girl she used to be would stay in her heart forever, if only as a reminder that she was now charmed and to never take it for granted. Be down to earth and kind was her mantra, but take no crap was firmly included in that mantra. Those defence walls would be staying up permanently. As the years ran by, she had her pick of men, and various boyfriends stole and broke her heart, and she broke many. She was always aware of time and how precious it was, and that happiness had to outweigh everything. It was imperative she got that right at least. Her older brother, Fionn, had drilled it into her over the years about how people only got one chance at life and not to squander it. He was an adrenaline junkie who revelled in everything to do with adventure and was the eternal optimist. His words would burn in her brain endlessly.

Nonetheless, despite that awareness at the forefront of her mind, time rolled by taking with it all the different jobs and courses, the wreckage she left behind, the beauty jobs following the course that never came to be, as she had decided she wanted something with meaning. Cafés, office work, call centres, bar work, pizza delivery... the list went on! They all resulted in her getting worse and staying only a day in some cases before escaping to her car, without saying a word to her new employer who might just catch a glimpse of her speeding off in her grey, Toyota Celica sports car. She was a free spirit, a bird who needed to keep exploring, flying around, observing people in every detail, collecting information on life, all the while lost, but free. She spent these years questioning herself constantly, always resilient, ready for the next fresh start, assuring herself she would get it right this time.

She was now twenty-one years old and found herself working as a Debt Collector in a Tool Hire business in the city suburbs. With her new long, blonde braided hairstyle, quirky style, striking looks, and a rebellious nature that was deepening within her more and more, she found herself ready, once again, to take on the world. She was the only girl in a sea of males in the office and quickly learned after a few too many sexist, disrespectful comments, that if she didn't whip them into shape and keep them in check, they would not respect her, and they would treat her like a blonde bimbo, so she played it friendly but tough. She would have to be on top, because she knew what it was to be on the bottom, and that wasn't an option. It was all guesswork on her part, always wading her way through the dark, making it up as she went along. She had figured different environments and various people required her to show a different version of herself, and all those roads always led back to the same road, survival. It was always about survival, but her plan worked.

Her male co-workers revelled in her spirited ways. They could see the softness underneath this tough tomboy exterior, sure it was written all over her, always being solid and kind, making sure they caught the end of fairness in all she did. Nevertheless, she was a tough cookie, and they watched in awe as she fearlessly went onto building sites collecting cheques with her head held high, conducting herself with laser-sharp focus, strength, class and grace but they also knew not to mess with her. She would face that fight to the death and never back down if she felt convinced of her truth. They also knew her as honest, loyal, feisty, stronger than any man, liberated, a brilliant worker, and a mighty good craic.

One afternoon, the lads were chatting about her in the canteen and an office worker, Jimmy piped in, 'We can have man talk all day and she doesn't bat an eyelid, and she never stops laughing at our jokes.'

Jimmy, an ex-Army man adored her and brought her coffee every day to her office. She thanked him profusely and he would laugh.

'Where do I cash that?'

'Cash it into the Bank of Adoration that I opened for you,' she would giggle.

Always charming and knowing just what to say to him and all the guys when she wanted to manipulate them, but the fondness that rolled between these two was a match made in heaven. He was short and heavyset with plenty of dark hair and big, dark, blue eyes, combined perfectly with a superb, heavy, black moustache all wrapped up in the kindest face you could hope for. He had a little edge too, though with his numerous tattoos, feisty spirit, and quick-witted comebacks. He had lived, that was for sure, and at forty years old now he was happily married with kids, but he just got Georgia and she got him in a perfectly platonic way.

On a rare occasion, he would even find her asleep behind her computer in her own private office, pretending she had her head buried in accounts, while nursing the hangover from hell. He watched her try to keep up with all the monthly targets and paperwork, chain-smoking, drinking endless amounts of coffee, and had seen her down Xanax on one or more occasions. Unbeknownst to her, he had caught her also on occasion staring out of her window, when she thought no one was looking and a serious, sad emptiness would fill up her face. An aching, far-away, worried look. In those moments it was like time stood still, and he thought he had her figured out, but he was wrong, there was more. He had zoned his eyes in more, a cold icy stare looking downwards with a sad mouth and her body still and stiff; like a window into her soul.

Why did she never look like that in front of them? What's going on there? It made him uneasy. In some ways he felt like she was his daughter and he was experiencing a real love for her. Seeing her like this was weird to him, and he promised himself he would keep a stronger eye on her. He wondered whether the pressure was getting to her, and on one rainy morning, coffee in hand and smile at the ready, he expressed his concern to her.

'I need to save to buy my own house. I can do it, if I just save up the money. Don't worry, I can handle it,' she said dismissively.

He knew his words had flown off into space, because he knew that look in her eye. She was a law unto herself, but a month later, when he watched her give work-experience to one of his co-worker's daughters, his heart melted. She had treated her like a daughter. She had surprised them all with that one, but Georgia explained, matter of factly to them, that when she had done her work experience in school, way back when in a hairdressing salon, that the girls had made a fool out of her and messed her up badly. She was going to make sure this girl had a great experience. She'd be damned if she were going to dole out the shabby treatment she had been given. Moments like these made her male co-workers feel they could almost touch the real her, but even so, she was like the street cat that had been battered over the years and was afraid to be touched in case it was beaten. Jimmy was just grateful he was privy to her most soft-hearted side more than any of the others, but he and the other guys had also seen her in action with some truck drivers, customers and especially with the manager who even the guys feared.

His name was Richie, and his Gordon Ramsey type temper and flair ups were daily. Richie secretly thought the world of her, but she was a challenge to him. He needed to be on top, not her. A confused work order brought it to a head one day with him being sure he would win this fight and let her know who was boss, but midway he had to back down and admit defeat. She had looked him right into his eyes with her steely glare and told him in a calm definite slightly husky voice.

'You will never talk to me like crap and get away with it. I'll stand before you every day and I'll make your wife look like Mother Teresa. I will bust your balls every minute.

I'll make it my life's mission until you learn how to treat me like a lady and with the respect I deserve. When you address me you will do that respectfully. I will die fighting you for my own honour. Not even my father could make me back down.'

He began to laugh.

'Do you know something? I adore you, you're a damn firework and we are lucky to have you.'

She flashed him a huge smile of approval and hugged him. All was forgiven. It was all in the rear-view mirror now. Control had been regained. In her mind, the captain had regained control of the ship, and she and Richie were to become firm friends. No one or nothing would stop her. She was her own judge and jury, but she knew damn well she was running out of chances and ideas and she was slipping. Things were starting to spiral downward, and she was well aware of the fact. By now, her three siblings were all successful in high-flying jobs and here she was a failure, somebody who just couldn't get it together. She spent thousands of hours soul-searching what was wrong. She needed to be a success and she wasn't going to do that in a Tool Hire. It would have to be bigger than that. She would tirelessly question herself as to whether she was too quirky, wilful, or just an odd pair of shoes in a world to which she didn't belong. No matter how deep she dug it remained a mystery to her.

Fast forward a couple of years, and now in her mid-twenties, depression had taken hold and the girl once nicknamed Smiley, smiled no more. Every chance she got, she wrapped herself up in her bed and slept and slept. She chain-smoked fags, got stoned, drunk and just frivolously let her life pass her by. Over time, she began to think suicidal thoughts every day. This would last for months. She supposed the only thing that stopped her crashing her car into a ditch was her loving, unbelievably kind, positive, humorous family, and the hope that a better life awaited her.

3

I blindly go where danger lurks

A romantic weekend trip to Paris was to put everything into perspective. A few hours after her arrival with her English boyfriend Mike, they got the subway to the Eiffel Tower. They had posed for a portrait on the bridge and had thought it was a dream come true. She was a die-hard romantic and being in Paris was literally blowing her mind. The cafés, the various sites, the tall quaint buildings, French language, it was all ahead of them. She loved every moment of it until tragedy struck on her way back to the hotel from the Eiffel Tower. She was cold and hungry and in her hurry to get to the other side of the pedestrian crossing, she rushed ahead of her boyfriend Mike. She quickly glanced to her left and was satisfied that the road was clear, but she was wrong. So wrong. Something hit her in the side, and at that very second she realised what was happening. She was being knocked down. It looked like a massive white car, with the headlights blazing and she was going to die. Everything happened just as they say it does, all in slow motion. Only seconds in time, but it felt like the longest minutes of her existence. She was tossed up into the air, like a rag doll and came crashing down on the ground, skidding along the cold, hard, rough tarmac, using her face and head as a break. She was aware the entire time going with the motion of getting killed.

Any second now, it would be lights out and she would go to heaven, but oh, the regret. She wasn't ready, God, no. A turn of events occurred in the shape of a second chance. She opened her eyes and looked up. The white car was stopped dead in the road in front of her, and a middle-aged French woman, crying and shouting for help stood before her. Her boyfriend was rushing to her side, freaked out crying, terrified at what lay before his eyes. *She was alive. Alive. How had she survived it?* She looked down at herself on what was now the other side of the road and thought, *oh my God, another car can come and knock me down again and finish the job this time.*

GET UP, GET THE HELL UP, she screamed in her head.

She peeled herself off the ground now realising her pants were at her ankles, and to make it worse she had forgone any underwear that day as the pants were so low rise. She grabbed her pants with her bloody torn hands and pulled them up regaining her dignity and rushed like a madwoman to the other side of the road. Her hair was standing as if she'd just got an electric shock. A tuft of hair was missing from her hairline as it had been ripped straight from her scalp by the force of her skid on the road. Her face was bloody and scratched and while her boyfriend hugged her tightly she just kept repeating.

'I'm alive, I'm alive, I love you, I love you,' in sheer disbelief that she had survived.

A French man who witnessed the accident came over to help her. He spoke softly and sympathetically trying to comfort this poor traumatised foreign girl in front of him. He could see the despair in her eyes, and though her boyfriend was holding onto her his heart felt like breaking for her. He sat on the kerb and reached out his hand to clasp hers, holding it reassuringly with kindness rebounding from his eyes deep into hers.

He's like an angel, she thought, as her boyfriend tried to ring an ambulance.

She knew he was French and they wouldn't be able to speak, but his actions consoled her to the deepest level. The hand of this perfect stranger was an angel in the dark, and underneath her crying, panicked shrieks lay a knowingness inside that it would be all ok. She would rise through it all, if only she could just stop crying. Shock filled her body and when the ambulance arrived and took her to the hospital she was informed she had broken her nose, but it would heal itself. Through a crowd of cold, uncaring doctors and a shoddy examination, stood a female nurse who helped her through it all, just like the stranger from before, and her boyfriend stayed diligently by her side.

'Pants off,' barked the impatient, heartless doctor in charge of her, to which she begged for a towel but nobody knew English. It seemed those two words by the doctor summoned up the extent of how much English he knew, as each word she spoke was met with a blank expression.

The female nurse relied on body language to understand and got her a towel to protect her dignity, while flooding her with kindness. At this point, she had been crying nonstop for hours and literally could not stop. A taxi ride back to the hotel with a speeding driver proved another blow to her already shattered fragile mind. She had been sent away from the French hospital with just paracetamol tablets for her injuries. Now back at the hotel, begging her boyfriend to get her cigarettes and alcohol, she began to examine herself. The top of her head and scalp were bouncy and felt like jelly. Her knees had blown up about four times their normal size, and she felt utterly battered and traumatised. She smoked and smoked and wondered if she slept would she ever wake again.

Did she have a concussion? She just knew that she hadn't been examined properly and paranoia flooded her thoughts. Eventually she lost the fight and fell into a deep slumber. The following day her mother, Jo rang wondering how the trip was going. Georgia did her best to raise her voice pitch and pretend all was fine, as she knew her mother was an Olympic worrier. It fell flat however as her mother was not swallowing that pill.

'Your voice is down in your boots, what's happened?'

This made Georgia slightly giggle in her head, as she was sure she had been speaking at her highest range.

God, what didn't that woman ever miss? Mystifying. Georgia persisted to tell her, she was having a ball but was just tired. Her mother had to accept she was getting nothing out of her but was extremely eager for her to get home. The hotel checkout day was Sunday, and the hotel staff ordered Mike and Georgia to vacate the room at 9 am. They had now been in Paris for three days, all of which she had spent in her bed recovering after the accident on Friday, their arrival day. Their return flight was not due until that evening, and even though the hotel staff had seen what had happened to her, they insisted she should wait in the lobby.

Heartless bastards would echo in Georgia's mind but she had bigger fish to fry. She figured this horror scene was going to scare the heck out of her family, and she wondered how she could soften the blow for them. While waiting in the lobby, a genius idea occurred to her, she could use the happy video footage that she had taken with Mike before the incident and tie it in with an after video of her being knocked down. This video would all be edited with her laughing about it, sarcastically stating all the wonderful things she hadn't done and that she would highly recommend anyone going there. She knew her tribe and they would hurt themselves laughing at this and quite honestly it took her mind off the pain and distracted her from the trauma. It was what her family always did, laugh in the face of life's most horrible moments.

That evening at Charles de Gaulle airport, a storm began to brew within her. She was now walking with a cane that Mike had got her, and she noticed aggressive-looking armed guards holding machine guns. She was feeling uneasy and couldn't wait to arrive home. As she stepped on to the plane she turned around to face France in all its non-glory and said in a quiet voice with narrowed eyes and a definite look,

'Goodbye Paris, you will never see me again. C'est la vie, my arse.'

She said these words with disdain. Somewhere within her, she felt vicious, resentful, and bitter at how her weekend had gone, but she quickly buried that voice because she knew it would only pull her down and she'd had enough of that. An air hostess approached her interrupting her thoughts and offered her a wheelchair for the flight. She graciously thanked her, but assured her that she would be responsible for her mother's early trip to the grave if she disembarked the plane in a wheelchair.

When she got home her mother and father were anxiously awaiting her arrival at the terminal. They were shocked to see their daughter black and blue, swollen, and walking with the help of a cane. Her mother thought she had been mugged, as did her father and horrified expressions filled their faces. Georgia's face lit up with the biggest smile, as she tried to wave reassuringly at them.

'Don't worry, I'm fine. It's all fine.'

'Jesus, what in the name of God?' her mother said.

'I was knocked down, but it's all good, I'm fine and I have a hilarious video for ye all. The before and after. Call the lads, and we will go and watch it and break down laughing.'

They knew this was a coping mechanism, so they followed her lead and that's just what they all did. They congregated in her parent's house, watched the video and broke down laughing. They found it so funny, they begged Georgia to show it to their friends.

'Go on,' she said, without a care in the world.

Hell. I'm alive, God damn it. Her mother insisted she stay with them for a few days, instead of returning to her one bedroomed flat in the city, while she nursed her better with her favourite food and magazines. She would however, feel troubled while she watched Georgia go into her Toyota Celica car to smoke a scary amount of cigarettes. Soon after, her mother Jo then took it upon herself to ring Georgia's employer to explain what happened, and even told him that Georgia's pants had been blown off and she hadn't been wearing underwear, which quite frankly, Georgia shuddered at.

The following week Georgia arrived back to work, walking extremely slowly and with a look of pain on her face. She was met by all the guys who worked with her at her Tool Hire job. The welcome they gave her literally touched her heart and she saw them in a light she had never done before. They couldn't believe that just over a week ago she had been taunting them with delight about her upcoming trip to Paris, and here she was now standing in front of them, looking like a wounded soldier. The caring, thoughtful actions they demonstrated towards her touched her deep inside. She was feeling the love.

Everything was different, the job looked different, her family, friends, and boyfriend. Something huge had changed in her, and she realised she had been terribly negative before all this. Now whether she liked it or not, this sickeningly positive happy person had emerged and if the truth be told she kind of liked it. She had always been a bit of a daredevil before Paris, testing the boundaries and asking people to drop her off in the middle of traffic in front of buses and cars, cocky as anything, thinking she was invincible, so on reflection she reckoned this was the wakeup call she needed.

Everything was becoming clearer, and over a casual breakfast one morning, out of nowhere, soon after the accident, she questioned Jo…

'Mum, can you fall out of love in just one day?'

Her mother looked at her puzzled.

'What do you mean love?'

'Well, I just realised that I woke up today and I don't love Mike anymore. I have only one goal and that is to break up with him as soon as possible.'

Her mother shocked, grilled her more, but she knew the story, Georgia would do what she wanted. If she made up her mind, forget it, don't even bother, and that's just what Georgia did in the blink of an eye. Even though they had spent two years together, she blindsided him and left him broken. She was the most warm, loving person you could ever meet but had a cold streak that if you found yourself at the end of it, God help you. You would feel like you didn't even exist, and even question whether you had imagined knowing her all along, because in her eyes she had left the building, and was no longer yours and never would be again. You were essentially dust. Upon reflection, she felt that Mike had been a very immature guy who had played it all the wrong way. He had taken her for granted, insulted her, played games, never valued her but enjoyed possessing and controlling her. She perceived that he did love her deeply but in his messed-up way. She didn't want to hurt him, but she had been given a second chance at life and plodding along wasn't going to be an option anymore.

With this new-found freedom, Georgia's head was in a spin. A few months had passed and on a glorious July day, Georgia jumped up suddenly off her chair in the office.

'I have to go lads.'

Her co-workers were bewildered.

'What do you mean Georgia? Where?'

'I have to leave lads. This bird has to go and fly onto new pastures.'

'But where?' her best buddy, Jimmy asked.

'To be honest I don't have a clue, but I'm not meant to be here anymore,' she bluntly replied.

In Georgia's mind, this had been the perfect time to announce her news, as most of the guys were in the shared office. They all looked up at her horrified, and she noticed the look on their faces and paused for a moment perplexed.

Why do they look hurt? Ah, it's because maybe they will miss me. She straightened herself and cleared her throat.

'Right, take two. Guys, you know me for speeches. I'm not a touchy-feely cringy girl, but I'll tell you once now, so listen up. I'm going to miss you all terribly. You are all like my extended brothers. Thank you for everything guys, and I mean it. I'll never forget you and I really hope I haven't been too much of a pain in the ass.'

Her eyes began to water. She hated to show emotion, but they could all see it.

One of them piped up, 'Hey who's this girl? We haven't met her before.'

She smiled softly with sincerity and looked them straight in the eye.

'No guys, she's been here all along, she was just hiding.'

Seven days later, she had worked out her notice, and on her final day she looked back behind her to face the building for the last time.

Screw the job and the building, but I'm going to miss those guys. She didn't like unfinished business. She had wanted to leave this job without feeling but realised you can't win them all. *Duty calls, it always calls, and she would just have to figure out what the duty was this time......*

4

With you my love, I'm singing in the rain

Fresh in the throes of figuring out her brand-new life, Georgia, together with her new best friend, Amelia, began to blaze her way through date after date and nights on the town. She had met Amelia through mutual friends and both girls were in the same boat entirely. Both single and ready to live it up. Georgia had always kept friends a little at arm's length, but Amelia had a way of dragging out the authentic Georgia. With their laid-back attitude and love of fun, the two girls went wild. Even though Georgia was having the time of her life, her love-life wasn't going according to plan. Every guy she met seemed only intent on bedding her without ever bothering to get to know the real her. She dated guys of many different backgrounds and careers, but their desire for her did not extend to her brain, only her body.

Needing men to notice her was an intrinsic part of her personality. Throughout her life she had been hurt and wounded, and although she had gone through a metamorphosis, and had come out a butterfly, the scars from those wounds of rejection and judgment from males were permanent. Yes, she was beautiful, and she could fly, but she found herself constantly looking to see who was noticing that she could do these things. Without an admirer or witness to her amazingness, it was like there was no point. She was still desperately insecure, and needed men to know that she was strong, beautiful, deep, complicated, multifaceted and kind. That is why she showed everyone glimpses of all the parts of her, but then she found herself running away because the effort of constantly being her best self was exhausting, so she found herself moving to the next job, next situation, next man to be an even better, stronger version of herself. She had cloaked herself in armour but unfortunately men were the chink in that armour.

Two years later with more failed jobs added to her belt, she started to feel that what had started out as so much fun and freedom was now starting to weaken her. She was becoming unhappy, drinking too much, and smoking too much weed, and quite frankly starting to lose control.

On a chance night out, she was living it up on the dance floor, and noticed a familiar face on the surround of the floor. She was very drunk, but not too drunk to connect the dots. This stunning guy with dark hair, blue eyes and a handsome face looked smiling in her direction.

She sauntered up to him.

'I remember you. I gave you a spin in my car many years ago.'

He chuckled heartily, lighting up.

'Yes, you did.'

She kissed his hand and flashed him that look… the look that said I want you. He clutched her in his arms and laughed with surprise.

'You're drunk, you just kissed my hand.'

'Did I? I can't believe I just did that.'

He assured her it was funny and suggested they get some air, so they walked through the city into the early hours talking, laughing, and flirting like crazy. He brought her home to his one-bedroom house in the city centre. By now it was 3 am, and Georgia, still in her blue, denim dress, fell asleep in his arms but not before making sure that he understood that this was no one night stand. As she began to sober up she remembered that he was a distant friend of her ex- boyfriend, one she had infatuated over at first sight while giving him a spin in her car. After telling him this, Jesse proceeded to tell her that he had noticed her long before the time in her car. It was at a party and she had overindulged on the booze but despite her intoxication he had been captivated by her. He knew, however he stood no chance as she was taken, but he had never forgotten her. They talked all night every night, and over the next few months they fell madly in love. He was like an angel sent down from heaven to Georgia and it was the first time a man wanted to know her properly. She was playing it safe, not giving too much away. It was like a game of chess for her. There could be no mess ups, or she would lose him, and she couldn't afford for that to happen. One day soon after that, while visiting her parent's, her father, Harry, noticed a glint in her eye as she sat in his armchair, lost in thought.

'A penny for your thoughts?'

'I want Jesse to know everything about me and vice versa. It will bring us even closer. He's the one Dad, I know it. He is what I've been waiting for.'

Her father broke down laughing.

'What's so funny?' she inquired, slightly offended.

'Oh my girl, have I taught you anything? If he knows everything about you, there will be no mystery, and for a man there must always be mystery. Only give him the bare amount and he will be yours. Trust me. Life is a game and you've got to learn how to play it Georgie.'

Georgia soaked up this information and smiled coyly.

'Yes, what was I thinking? You are right.'

'I've been telling you for years, have I not?' smiled Harry.

'I guess you have actually.'

At that moment, life became a game to Georgia, and she intended to become a shrewd player. Jesse was the yin to Georgia's yang and at twenty-nine years old, he was four years older than her and fresh out of a three-year broken relationship. He was enjoying singledom and was in no hurry to take on another girlfriend. He had wrestled in his mind with how to handle this new situation that for him had come a little too early, but he just knew deep down, that if he let her go, he would never have her again. She had let him know in her cheeky way that he either wanted in or out. She wasn't going to be second best or one of his many women. He liked that about her. The way she would put her cards on the table and gamble and risk the one thing she didn't want to lose, him.

He could feel her intense love from the start, without her even breathing a word. She was strong as a lioness and he had never met anyone like her, ever. He acknowledged yes she was wreckless and wild, but she was also a million different things. When he was in her presence he came to life. Everything became exciting with her around. He felt like he could just die with joy when she laughed with-out inhibition and her freeness untied him from his own chains. With her by his side they could light up the world together.

He figured she just had to stay, and with that he let her in to the deepest part of him. Her spell had been cast and he fell deeply in love with her. In the dead of the night he would sometimes feel his chest pound at the overwhelming feelings she had unearthed in him. Over time Georgia knew it was in the bag and started to relax and let Jesse see the real her. No matter what she said or did, he wouldn't bat an eyelid and she felt freer than ever. She was always doing something, up all night, passionately working on her latest idea or creation but also in stark contrast he would find her staring out the window at nature for hours, quiet as could be and deep in thought. She was a complex character and it came naturally to him to just take her as he found her. Jesse was the kind of guy who was chilled, no matter if the house was burning down around him. He was content to work at the local bakery every day, but nonetheless was always eager for the clock to strike 6 pm, so that he could come back to her once again.

Six months later, they moved in together, and every day they would wake up next to each other smiling and laughing, ready for their next adventure. Her quirky ways kept him on his toes, and she continued to change like the wind. Among her many passions was art & design and one evening when he came in from work, she showed him some shoe designs she had been working on. She had managed to fill a sketch pad full of designs in only a few short hours. Another night, he would watch her paint the entire house just because she said it needed to be done. She was highly creative and so was he, so it just worked. They were both such free spirits they decided not to marry or have kids. They would just shoot the breeze and laugh their way into oblivion. Georgia believed that if you didn't have a desperate longing for a baby, then you probably had no business having a child, and while there were fleeting thoughts of children, the feeling wasn't powerful enough to take such a leap. Jesse felt that their lives were complete already and had no desire to have children together. He had watched his parents divorce as a child and wanted to take a different road in life. While Georgia acknowledged that she would love a wedding, she knew that was quite the exchange for a life of commitment. It didn't feel right for either of them but they were perfectly committed in their minds. Georgia knew now what it was to have a partner in crime, and no matter where she went or what she did, she knew she had someone waiting at home who loved her and accepted her for all her colours.

She proved to Jesse over time that she would be his guardian angel too. This promise was put to the test one night while on the way home from a trip to the shops. A man followed them down an alley threatening to attack them. Jesse pushed her behind him, ready to protect her and fight this lunatic. She pushed his hand out of the way and glared at him.

'If he jumps us, I will fight him with you. There's no way I'm standing back. You can forget it. You take on one of us, you take on both of us. I'll fight him to the death with you and I'll fight him like a man.'

He looked into her glaring eyes and with her fists raised and clenched and her militant, facial expression, he just knew he had no choice. He knew that in the past she had learned to protect herself. She had dabbled in Karate and boxing, earning herself a brown belt and even sparred with her older brother's friends in her youth. When alone living in a scary shithole, she had one time gone to bed so scared that she had placed a hammer under her pillow, ready to defend herself if necessary before doing whatever it took to get out of that unsafe place. She was a survivor, and when the fight or flight impulse kicked in, she had learned to stand and fight.

She's small but Christ, when it comes to protecting the ones she loves, she is fearless.

'Come down and watch us destroy you,' she screamed to the guy in the alley.

Jesse had his legs apart and fists in the air saying the same thing.

'Make my fucking day. Get down here.'

They were ready for anything, united to save each other. Two of them against the world. The scumbag could see the craziness before him and decided to run away. Georgia and Jesse could not believe it had not come to a fight. The adrenaline filled their bodies, their breathing now so loud with the sheer fear of how close they had come. Jesse looked at Georgia who was still on the highest alert possible. He observed how her face looked slightly distorted and unfamiliar as it was so scrunched with temper, fear and stress.

'It's okay. We're safe. Let's go home and get a drink. Christ almighty,' sighed Jesse, trying his best to regulate his breathing back to normal.

'I thought I'd have to help you kick some ass there. Jaysus, my heart. I think I just lost a few years off my life there, the little bastard,' replied Georgia, still wound up to the last.

Georgia tuned into the blood rushing feverishly through her veins, her chest tight and restricted, and the tears pricking her eyes. She had become accustomed to these feelings over the years, and sometimes she wondered if her fight response was always just barely below the surface, barely contained.

They had come across trouble before, on the rare occasion and events like these only served to strengthen their bond. They were inseparable. Apart from the rare bad experience which Georgia referred to as 'just life', these years were like respite for Georgia, and she believed she had unlocked the secret to happiness, not just in terms of love, but in relation to her career also. She had enrolled in a social science degree course as a mature student, and everything was going dandy. Life was looking pretty darn good for Jesse and Georgia until one by one, the wheels started to come off the fairytale cart.

She was so busy enjoying life that she was doing little or no study for University and handing in below-par assignments. One day the course co-ordinator beckoned her to his office. As she walked inside, she noticed two other senior lecturers sitting beside him. In a serious tone she was told, in no uncertain terms that she was failing the course, and they did not feel she had what it would take to pass the end of year exams. Georgia never saw it coming and realised they were right. For these last couple of years she had her head in the sky, but now she was back on earth with a thud. She immediately knew she had to fight this decision and save herself. It was only last week she had been joking with Jesse about all the money she was going to make when she had completed the course.

'We'll be rich,' she had declared, and they had laughed themselves silly at the thought.

Now the smile had been firmly wiped from her face. With a panicked expression, she pleaded with the lecturers to be sympathetic towards her.

'You are right, I've messed up, I hold my hands up but I beg you all, just give me one more chance and I will get a second-class honour.'

It seemed a bit silly to pretend she would get a first-class honour, as even she knew she wasn't willing to swat that hard. They shook their heads. It wasn't working. Her trusted charm was broken. She swallowed hard, half-defeated and summoned the strength within her to try again.

In her scattered mind, she willed herself, *this time bring it home*.

'Please. You have no idea what this means to me. I will get on the floor in front of you and beg on my hands and knees. There's nothing I won't do. You must believe me, just take a chance. Look in my eyes. I have learnt my lesson and I'm sorry beyond belief. You gave me this place in the course and I blew it, I know I did, but I want to be a Psychotherapist and I'm going to make you proud, if you just let me.' With her mouth still open, fumbling for words the Head of the Department stopped her.

'Ok, ok, this is your last chance. One more strike and you are out.'

The fellow lecturers agreed reluctantly. Georgia thanked them profusely and went home to her boyfriend. This whole wakeup call had really taken it out of her. She filled Jesse in on what had happened and told him with the most serious and determined face he had ever seen on her that she was going to study like a mad woman. She could not mess this up. Fun and games were over. She had one year to make up for three years and she needed that 2:1. It was all about the 2:1 now. If she could get this mark in her exams, the sky was the limit. Jesse agreed to support her and watched her go to work. True to her word, night and day she studied. She had never studied like this in her life, and at times she would admit to Jesse she worried she was going mad, but she kept on at it and it became her life's mission. When Georgia was on a mission nothing else existed and you just stayed the hell out of her way. As the year came close to completion Georgia felt she had finally caught up with her studies and a new sense of spirituality began to develop in her. She confided in Jesse that she felt her deceased Nana, her life-long guardian angel had been helping and inspiring her from start to finish. There's no way she could have done it all by herself. It was that big.

Exam day beckoned, and she kept her focus and gave it everything she had. She was feeling seriously confident and her dreams of Psychotherapy were shining big and bright in her mind. She wished away the summer that followed the exams, dying with excitement to see her results. Patience never was her strong point, but the day finally arrived. Her sister Sophie, a college lecturer of Philosophy, was with her when the envelope arrived.

'You open it, I can't,' she gestured to her sister.

'Are you sure?' Sophie asked.

Georgia nodded and there it was. The 2:1 she had put her soul into, right there on paper. She jumped up and down and nearly knocked her sister over as she hugged her with delight. She was so proud and she had made her parents proud. This was such an achievement, she had seen it through, pushed herself harder than she ever had. She slumped to the ground, holding that sheet of paper close to her heart, unsure whether she was going to burst into tears or laughter.

As the days passed, Jesse noticed a change in Georgia's mood. Her elation seemed to give way to a sense of apathy.

He wondered what had happened to the ecstatic Georgia who had got what she wanted.

He sat down beside her and asked gently, 'What's up?'

'I've had an epiphany.'

'Right?' said Jesse, bewildered.

'I don't want to go to my graduation. I've had a good think about the Psychotherapy, and I don't want that either. I want none of the jobs the course has to offer.'

Jesse sat there looking shocked and Georgia went on to explain.

'On reflection, I think I just had to prove to everybody that I'm smart. Job done, nobody can ever again call me dumb. I don't belong in that world of Social Science, I just don't. Time to go back to that stupid drawing board.'

Her eyes welled up with tears and a look of sadness enveloped her.

'I'm a winner but I'm a failure and do you know what? I must be cursed. All that damn work and look where we are now. Nowhere,' said Georgia, tearfully.

Jesse leaned in to comfort her, but he knew nothing he could say would bring her round. He would have to let her sit it out her own way and just be there when she needed him. For the next few weeks her downer would continue. When graduation day came her only reason for showing up was due to the pleas of her family, but they all knew that dream was over and she was back to square one.

5

Test me to the ends of time, for I shall find
stars in the darkest sky

On a windy night as she lay back on the couch watching the TV, she saw a story pop up that grabbed a hold of her insides. It was a news story of a woman throwing a cat in a bin. Her face turned to thunder as she listened to all the details, and she took it upon herself to look up the details of the story online. As she researched the story, she accidentally came across other animal abuse stories and a fire lit within her. She felt she had to do something about it.

'Look, look, Jesse. Look what's going on in the world. Have we been sound asleep? Oh my God,' gasped Georgia.

Jesse could see her distress and agreed it was awful.

Georgia couldn't get it out of her mind, and all she knew is she had to do something, anything to help. A new purpose was born, and she started to sign petitions.

'It's not enough,' she would cry.

She was already a vegetarian because of a book on weight loss which she had read two years previously. This book contained some disturbing information on the meat industry and after reading it, she announced to Jesse that she was intent on becoming a vegetarian.

'I'm vegetarian now.'

He had looked at her stunned.

'Where did that come from?' he asked. 'You were a meat eater going into the bath and now you have come out a vegetarian.'

'Well, that diet book, called Skinny Bitch, that I was reading is pro-vegetarian. I'll never eat meat again. Just watch,' she said.

Jesse sat there with his mouth agape.

He should be accustomed by now to her impulsive ways but she always managed to shock him all the same.

'My Georgie, the whirlwind,' he replied, supportively upon hearing her news.

She had always wanted to be a vegetarian and ate little meat as it was, but she had been convinced by doctors along the way that she would run into bad health without it. She had lived on brown bread and bananas for the early part of her childhood years but different doctors warned her she would get into bad health if she didn't change her diet. She had also regularly cried into her dinner as a child when meat was served up, and she would look at her mother with sad eyes and ask, did this have a life? It was always written in the stars, but this time she promised herself she would do it right and eat all the right things to stay strong.

Two moody weeks passed after seeing the animal news story, with Georgia racking her brain as to how she could help more. She then stumbled onto an idea that she would find an animal activist group and join them. She went on to become firm friends with the girl in charge. They spent their time rallying people and encouraging them to turn up at events and campaigns. She quickly became aware of a whole host of animals causes, ranging widely from seal hunting, fox hunting, fur farms and animal act circuses. The list was endless, and she was finally using her skills in a way she had always planned, helping animals.

Jesse continued to support her by coming along to most rallies and protests. He would playfully giggle at her when she would find a dying bird and bring it home to die peacefully in their yard in case a cat got to it, or when she would steal the angel from the Christmas tree to bury with a dead pigeon. In Georgia's mind this was perfectly normal behaviour and a show of respect. She would torture herself by enduring videos of animal cruelty so that she could identify with their pain and fully realise the horror of human capabilities.

Georgia was always a deep person but during this time that depth took over and became all of her. She began to lose a lot of weight and felt permanently stressed, and Jesse asked her if she should back off a little but she felt she had to be loyal to the animals, and carry on. She believed that whatever she was feeling was nothing compared to the suffering of the animals out there. Campaigns and protests were planned, and she pushed herself to the limit for the cause. When journalists asked her to pose at the front line she did it, even though she considered herself a background type person who didn't like attention.

She knew her looks would help get exposure for the cause and loved that they could serve the most important purpose to her. If the cause required her to pose in her underwear and end up on the newspaper to get exposure for the cause, she would do it, even though nothing else in the world could make her do that. Georgia was a private person who didn't like to expose herself to the world, physically or emotionally, but for this cause she could make herself go against her grain. The people who campaigned with her felt like kindred spirits and in them, she was met with her own reflection. She marvelled at their kindness, dedication and commitment to the cause, and knew the respect she had for them would never wane, not even when time would turn her old and grey. Among them were mothers, fathers and children who stole time from their lives in an attempt to forge a better world for the animals they loved to their core. It was never easy for any of them. Sometimes things got a little hairy, and when the public were aggressive with Georgia calling her names and a fanatic, she shrugged it off. This continued for just over a year, and by now Georgia had turned dark and the sky was falling in. All the strain had built up in her and she began to assess the approach she and the other animal activists were using to communicate their message. After much deliberation, she decided that she still completely believed in the cause and all the issues but she knew it was draining her and taking every ounce of energy both physical and mental out of her so she had to opt out. She felt ravaged from the entire experience yet she acknowledged there had been many victorious moments along the way. It was time for her to get out and she needed to save herself from drowning in the process. Weeks passed in a blur with Georgia growing extremely quiet. She was feeling guilty and burdened that she had left the group and felt she had abandoned the animals. She threw herself into her new blog Animal Education. Here she attempted to educate people on the plight of animals. This experience had changed her, and she grew more serious and withdrawn as the time went on, bouncing from job to job, and failing miserably.

At this stage, she was thirty-one years old, and in an attempt to stave off depression, she decided to start a Japanese postgraduate course in the local University. After a few months this course went off the road with all the others. Things were becoming strained with Jesse, and she felt as if someone had come along and blown out the candle of their love. They had been through so much together over the years, it had now begun to tear them apart from each other. Romance became non-existent and they began to communicate less and less.

In November, Georgia decided that she should attend her brother, Fionn's wedding in Fiji alone, and give them both time to think. It was a beach wedding, just the type of wedding she had imagined as a young girl. The dream that would never come to be. As she stood barefoot, with the water swaying in and out between her toes, she thought about Jesse. It was the most romantic, heartfelt ceremony, and as she listened to the waves crash and felt the sand on her feet and the sun warming her face, it became clear to her that their love had been swallowed up and had died.

When she returned from her trip, they both sat down for the chat they had been avoiding, and admitted to each other that this love story had come to an end. They both agreed that they had a hugely strong bond, and they would continue to be in each other's lives forever more, but as friends. They both knew deep down that they had become like brother and sister.

'I'll always be here for you Jesse, until you are old and grey, even if I meet somebody down the line. You are like my blood now.'

'I've always got your back too George, always.'

They hugged and cried about the demise of their once beautiful relationship, but both knew they had to go forward. It was for the best. Georgia decided she would move out and find a one bedroomed house in the city centre. This was a huge leap for her, as she had become so used to having someone by her side for all these years. She had met Jesse when she was twenty-five and they had been together for six years. When she considered the enormity of their parting, her brain literally could not conceive this change, and denial took over. Yes, this was a change she wanted but it was huge, and over time she would have to break it down in her head. She went straight into autopilot and found a small one-bedroom terraced house by the river in Cork city centre. She put her one unique stamp in the new place placing colourful curtains with butterflies and hanging her favourite items to make it feel like home but she needed a new focus. She was lonely and desperately needed a distraction from her painful break up. One morning while sipping her much loved coffee while looking out at the littered streets outside her window, she came across an ad for a music course, and applied for the course without delay. Days later, her application was accepted. The processing of the breakup would have to come later.

One evening, while at home and on a lengthy telephone call with her brother Oscar, she was hit by a bombshell. Oscar had been studying Autism as part of his work as a Psychologist and he gently told Georgia that he believed she may have mild Autism. He explained that autism was a spectrum disorder with Asperger's being high functioning at the mildest end of the spectrum. He had been taking classes and learning all about it, and Georgia kept running through his mind as his lecturer spoke.

He and Georgia were super close and had always shared their deepest feelings with each other. Georgia admitted to him that this had never crossed her mind whatsoever, and while she appreciated his opinion, she couldn't fathom it as a possibility. She knew he only had her best interests at heart, but this news threw her completely. She assured Oscar, she would give it some thought.

She started her music course and some days while walking up there, she would put on her headphones and listen to the angriest music she could find, while tossing Oscar's words over and over in her mind. Each time she tried to explore it, her brain would feel like it would explode. It was too much to handle, just like the breakup, it would have to keep, and she consoled herself with the fact that maybe her brother was wrong.

Nothing was official, not until she would get tested and that would be whenever she wanted, if at all, maybe years away. She would have to compartmentalise and just focus on the task at hand, the music course, and that's just what she did. After a couple of weeks at the course, Georgia began to make good friends with all her classmates, half of whom were also her smoking buddies at break time. She made it her business to be nice to everyone, but of course she had her favourites, especially Ben. He was about 5ft 8", had chin-length, long, blonde hair peppered with grey, and blue eyes with a kind smile. He was forty-seven years old and was completely on Georgia's wavelength. He loved to laugh, talk a lot, and was just a positive, enthusiastic guy. She had never cared about anyone's age, once she had a good rapport with them. Ben and Georgia pretty much went everywhere together, collecting new friends from the class as they went, and over time he convinced her to take up singing classes.

Georgia had always been an exceptional singer but very shy about it. Her parents had told her since she was young that she had a gift, but she would only sing around her family and she had to turn her back to them as she sang. Her father was a professional singer and had taught her that when you sing, you should pronounce every word like you mean it and feel it. He had a talent himself and sounded like Jim Reeves, and she recognised that people loved his singing because of his sincere, soothing tone and how he put such beauty into all of his words, and she figured that is how he captivated them. It all sounded so heartfelt and genuine when he sang, and she emulated this with her singing, putting beauty into every word. As the words would leave her mouth, she could hear the depth of her own voice and felt like she was exposing her heart, because as she sang, she would think of something or someone that had meaning for her.

After a while, she found that she couldn't sing other than with all her heart. She had decided, long before this music course, that this gift would have to stay hidden, because she couldn't expose her feelings. She reconciled with the thought that not every gift had to be showcased, but Ben was persistent. He felt nervous about doing these singing classes alone and needed support from his new buddy, Georgia.

After a few days of relentless pleading and doing his best to charm her, she gave in and went to meet her new singing teacher, Maya. She was short and slim, with fiery, red hair and big green eyes, and looked like a free spirit type. She was twenty-five years old and had a lot of life experience, having trained in London as an Opera Singer. She was full of positivity, confidence and enthusiasm and Georgia was pleasantly surprised with this outgoing, fun, new teacher. She explained to Maya that while she was a very confident person, when it came to singing she was very shy. Maya was sitting at her piano in the large room full of instruments. The super high ceilings and oversized windows generously allowed the sun to bombard the room with its rays.

'It's just you and me Georgia. The door is closed and nobody can hear us. There's a long hallway between this room and the other classes, and trust me, they can't hear anything. Just sing me a song, you have nothing to lose.'

With that, Georgia agreed that she would sing 'Missing You' by Des'ree. She decided to open up and give this song her full ability and as she sang, Maya's face changed from smiling to pensive. Maya was a first-class singer herself and could reach the highest of notes, and truly wasn't expecting much from this new girl Georgia, but she ended up being blown away. When Georgia finished the song Maya gazed at her in awe.

'Good God Georgia. I just got goosebumps and the hair is standing on my neck right now. You have one of the most impressive voices I have ever heard. There's so much depth in it. You went from low to high and there's so much colour in your voice, with all different strands. One minute its sounds chocolately, if that's even a word, and other times sweet like an angel.' Maya couldn't stop herself as she was feeling passionate about this girl's voice, which had come out of nowhere.

'Now listen to me Georgia, you have the best voice in this course and you could go somewhere with this.'

Georgia was blown away completely. She knew she had a good voice but this was downright unexpected. She thanked Maya sincerely.

They both continued with the lessons over the coming weeks, and with Maya's help, Georgia's skills improved greatly, and her talent began to soar. The singing was becoming Georgia's main focus, and then a new student named Sid started in her class. He was Scottish and full of colour. He was thirty-five, slim, tall and wore mad clothes and had a talent for shaking things up with his mere presence. He was rebellious, spoke his mind and completely liberated and Georgia loved that. He brought in his ukulele to class one day and Georgia had commented on how great he sounded and how much she had always wanted to play the instrument. They gelled immediately, like kindred spirits, with their common traits of feistiness and rebelliousness. He taught her how to play the ukulele in the canteen when they had spare time and she began practising at every opportunity. When she heard or played the ukulele, the sweet, bright sound seemed to have the magic power to enchant her, and wash all of her troubles away, if only for a while. It invoked just one feeling in her, and that was unadulterated happiness.

Music had now taken over her life and she just kept her focus on that solely. She shut out the breakup and every other problem and just kept herself distracted. On a dark, rainy night while she looked out of her window, she saw the stray cats she had been feeding and decided to write a song about them. She adored these cats, but they had caused her great distress. The neighbourhood she was now living in was one of constant stress and turmoil and full of anti-social behaviour.

These cats Tabby and Whitey were being chased by dogs, and also at times by young, rough tearaway kids. She was doing everything she could to keep them safe, but knew her landlord would never agree to having them in the house. She had already cried to her neighbour, Eddie, a fellow cat lover earlier that day when he told her one of the stray cats had been killed by some delinquent kids and their dog. Eddie had never seen this side of her personality. He had only seen her as the girl next door; tough and able to handle whatever life threw at her, so he came by and knocked on her door. When Georgia opened the door, she was gobsmacked to see her neighbour Eddie with a dead salmon in his hands and a beaming smile.

'I got this for you,' said Eddie, smiling.

'Oh, I don't know what to say, thank you Eddie but I'm a vegetarian,' said Georgia, in shock at the awkwardness of the situation, knowing full well he was just trying to be kind.

'Whaat, you are turning down a Salmon? Do you know how hard it is to get one of these?' asked Eddie, flabbergasted.

'I didn't, but I think I do now. Thank you Eddie, from the bottom of my heart, but I can't accept it,' said Georgia, feeling bad for Eddie.

'I didn't know you were a vegetarian. It upset me to see you cry earlier, and I just wanted to do something nice for you.

'You've got some heart on ya Eddie, do you know that? Thanks so much and I'm sorry I can't accept it. I swear I'm ok now. Don't worry about me,' said Georgia, with her heart beaming, at the kindness of Eddie.

'Can I give you a hug?' asked Eddie.

'Er, I'm not a big hugger, but as it's you yeah, give me a hug, you big softie.'

With that she wrapped her arms around him and hugged him tightly.

'Thank God for people like you Eddie. I wish I could clone you,' said Georgia, warmly.

'You're a pet, and don't worry, your secret is safe with me. I know it's a tough neighbourhood, and they don't need to know what a sweet girl you are under all that toughness, but I know,' said Eddie, walking away.

'Thanks Eddie,' glowed Georgia, as she closed the door, still smiling.

She knew Eddie had watched her over the months chase away undesirables, stick up for the cats numerous times, and put herself in danger for their safety. She felt downright touched by this heartfelt moment they had shared at her door, but it had made her emotional. She needed to release some of the hurt, fear and frustration that had been pent up inside her for so long, so she took up the ukulele in her arms and began to let the words flow....

Short Instrumental
♫

Baby, baby, baby,
Sitting on down,
You look at me with big eyes
All I do is frown

They don't see you like me
They don't see your charm
They don't see your heart
Coming on down

Chorus
O oo ooooooo
Baby, baby, baby
They're taking me down
Ooo ooooooo
Baby Baby Baby
They're taking me down

And I will be here for you till the end
I will stand, I will fight, all I can my friend
And I'll hold you dear, I will take you with me
I'm not always strong
So, I'll do what I can

Ooo ooooooo

Baby, baby, baby,
They're taking me down
O ooo ooooooo
Baby Baby Baby

They're taking me down
Down.

♫

After she finished singing she sobbed her heart out, relieving all the stress within her. When she dried her eyes she realised this was the first song she had ever written, and she was excited to share it with her closest friends in the music course. It took her a few days to pluck up the courage, but the right time presented itself when she was in the college messing around with Ben and Sid as they had been granted a free class. Sid had just belted out his own song and began to tease Georgia.

'Psst, what about you kid, do you have a song for us?'

'Yeah actually I do. It's called Baby, Baby, Baby.'

'Ok, good, said Ben. 'Let's hear it.'

Just as she began to sing, a figure entered the room.

6

Be still my heart, for you shall be pierced with
beauty that you have not yet seen

A t this point Georgia was already mid-flight and had
no choice but to continue. As she sang, she felt a ner-
vousness and a feeling of electricity strike her body at the
sight of the dark-haired man standing in the doorway. He
came into the room expecting his saxophone class was being held there, but quickly realised he had got it wrong.
He was pleasantly surprised to hear Georgia singing this
engaging song and for a few moments he forgot himself
and stood there transfixed listening to her voice.

There she is, that stunning girl I saw a month ago, on
what he reckoned was her first day at the smoking area. He
hadn't seen her since that day, as he had to take time out
to care for his father, who had recently suffered ill health.
Now here she was again in front of him. He didn't recognise the song she was singing and figured it must be
her own. *Woah, she sings and writes her own material. I'm in
heaven.* His mouth was slightly agape and he felt his chest
heave a little with the energy exuded by Georgia. He was
standing tall, still and glued to the ground beneath him,
temporarily paralysed by her beauty, talent and presence.

Georgia was singing from her soul, connected with every word she sang, whilst also feeling this wild chemistry between her and this perfect stranger. She couldn't help but notice that he looked captivated by her and a rush of excitement ran through her body. Now and then, their eyes would meet, and everything else in the room would fade into the background, and she would have to force herself to look away. He was just her type to a tee, but she knew she had to stay cool.

Ben and Sid looked dumbfounded at Georgia and Sid piped up,

'Gosh that was powerful! We never heard you sing before, what was the song about?'

Ben expressed the same interest.

'If I told you that I'd have to kill you, and let's face it, I like you too much for that,' laughed Georgia, gleefully.

She knew better than to tell the guys what the song was about. She knew damn well they wouldn't get it, and she also knew how to play the game, and how much to divulge to anyone in the college, even her friends.

'Alfie, you are looking pretty dazed there buddy,' called out Ben.

Alfie quickly noticed himself and came back down to earth with a bang.

'Oh, yeah. I was just confused as to where my saxophone teacher was. I thought we were meeting here.'

He was desperately trying to look cool, and cover over the fact that he had been staring at Georgia this entire time with a doe eyed expression. He felt embarrassed and exposed, and much as he tried to conceal his nerves, he knew it was obvious to Georgia and the two guys that he had been watching her intensely all this time. He looked nervously at Georgia.

'Sorry to interrupt your session, I didn't mean to intrude, you were sensational just there.' Georgia felt her cheeks redden and got all nervous with the compliment Alfie had just given her.

'Oh, thank you, that's really kind of you.'

She could feel her heart beat faster and really didn't know what else to say. Alfie quickly excused himself.

'Anyway, catch ye guys later.'

'Yeah,' said Georgia, 'See you around.'

She attempted to compose herself in front of Ben and Sid, looked at her watch and told the guys she had to go back to class.

That was uncomfortable, but thrilling. She hadn't seen this Alfie before. He wasn't in her class. She reckoned he must be in one of the other courses that ran downstairs. Later in the day it was time for tea break, and Georgia headed to the smoking area for her treasured cigarette and coffee. She was very surprised to see Alfie there among the other guys. She felt her heart begin to flutter again.

Twice in one day. I'm going to have to gather myself. He was standing against the wall with a cigarette in his hand looking all handsome. She had no choice but to stand next to him as there wasn't much room in the smoking area.

'Hi again. We haven't met officially yet, I'm Georgia.'

'Pleased to meet you,' replied Alfie, and they shook hands.

'Are you doing one of the courses downstairs? I haven't seen you out here before.'

'Yeah, I am. I've been here for the last year actually and I'm in the class across from the canteen.'

Georgia instantly picked up on an accent.

'Ah, I hear an accent there, where are you from? It's not from Cork anyway. Don't tell me, let me guess' …

He smiled widely in response.

'Mayo?'

'No, but good try! I'm from Galway. I'm Alfie by the way.'

They talked briefly about the music course, both slightly stumbling over their words and acting a bit awkward, and Georgia excused herself eventually to go back to class. She secretly hoped she would meet him again and he was certainly thinking the same. Meanwhile, Alfie was in a fluster after their talk. He was totally intrigued and so delighted she had broken the ice with him, because he didn't think he could have plucked up the courage to speak to her first.

He was now back in class and completely distracted as their conversation kept running through his mind. He pondered on how natural and easy to talk to she seemed to be, if he could just get his nerves under control. He loved the way her body moved, the way her hair bounced as she walked, the way she sat so straight in the chair as if she had taken the teacher's warnings 'to sit up straight' so literally all those years that she had carried the perfect posture into adulthood. *What kind of a girl was she?* he chuckled to himself. Here, he was daydreaming about why she sat that way, stood that way, whether the rogue strands that had escaped her hairbun were her natural colour. *What was she doing to him?* His intention to give up cigarettes was now thrown out the window as he planned on being out in that smoking area every day. He had to see her at every opportunity.

This music course had been going really well all along for Alfie, but everything had peaked now after meeting Georgia. The intensity of his attraction to her caught him totally unawares. Yesterday, she was a complete stranger and today seeing her seemed to be the only thing that mattered. He couldn't understand where this chemistry was coming from and why he was so drawn to her. The following day he made it his business to forget about eating at small break and he went straight through the canteen out to the smoking area. There she stood again up against the cold stone wall in the corner, talking to her teacher.

'Hi Georgia.'

His eyebrows raised unnaturally as he felt under pressure and unsure of himself.

'Oh, hi Alfie,' said Georgia, in a confident, breezy tone. 'Top of the morning to ya.'

With that she let out a hearty laugh.

'Jesus, I haven't heard that expression in about twenty years, haha.'

He pretended to tip his imaginary cap.

'Top of the morning to you too my good lady.'

Gee, she is good craic this one. She had put him at ease with her entertaining greeting.

'So, what have you on today,' asked Georgia.

'Oh nothing major. My class is just practising for a concert.'

'That sounds like fun and what are *you* doing for the concert?'

'Well,' revealed Alfie, 'I'm singing one song, and playing the saxophone for another.'

'What song are you singing?'

'Em, I'm singing 'Dancing on my own' by Calum Scott and I'm playing the saxophone for 'Born to run' by Bruce Springsteen.'

'Wow,' blurted Georgia, 'I love both of those songs. When are you having the concert? I'll have to hear them.'

'In about three weeks time, you should come,' replied Alfie, keenly.

'Yeah, now that I can't miss,' said Georgia, excitedly and flirtatiously.

With that she turned her attention to her teacher, Lewis who was now becoming a good friend of hers and proceeded to ask him his news. She was chatty, open, and friendly and knew how to work a crowd. She'd had plenty of practice over the years. Meanwhile, Alfie did his best to look cool, casual, and relaxed, smoking his cigarette. His head was in a spin again and his heart was pounding.

Jesus, am I sweating right now? Wow it's hot out here, but it was still only early Spring. He was gobsmacked she was so interested in what he had to say.

Oh my God, she said she will come to the concert. I'm going to blow her away. Time to get practising, he plotted in his mind. Break ended and he headed back to class and Georgia did the same. While back at her class, Georgia's mind began to trail off. She was thinking of Alfie and their chat earlier. She smiled coyly after analysing the approach she had used with Alfie. In her mind she had managed to look confident, at ease and friendly and didn't give any game away to him. He would soon see that she was nice to everyone, and then he wouldn't be able to distinguish whether she liked him or not.

Yeah, this is not my first rodeo, I will keep you guessing at all times. I'll take you on a wander down the garden path, and I'll show you how this game is played. He was a happy distraction from her problems, and she felt it was time to have some fun. For the next few weeks Georgia and Alfie continued to meet every day on their small break. By now she was on familiar terms with everyone, and she had found her feet. She always liked to cut straight through the awkwardness with people, and just dive in, without the small talk. Some days she would say hi to Alfie and proceed to have a brief conversation, going back and forth about topics such as music and what they did for the weekend. Other days she would purposely say hi and not engage in a chat and put her focus on the other students. Alfie felt he had to follow her lead and assumed she was just this popular girl. He would just have to take the back seat at times and not get her attention. It niggled at him a little, but he assured himself that he would win her over yet.

There was plenty of time, and he had heard that she had recently broken up with her boyfriend after a six-year relationship. He knew this might have to be a slow burner to give her a chance to heal, and he would wait, by God he would, however long. He would watch her out the corner of his eye every day and angle his body in her direction, to give her ample, opportunity to speak with him, and of course, to observe her every move. He would watch as she lit up the room wherever she went. Her kindness and laughter were infectious. He loved the way she gave her full attention to whoever she was speaking with. Both men and women were drawn to her. She was genuine and warm but also unpredictable and aloof. He savoured the sound of her laughter, especially her naughty laugh, and could never keep himself from smiling as he played it back throughout the day in his mind.

Does she like me though? He would wonder. She was nice to everybody. He would watch for signs of interest from her, and he couldn't say with conviction she was giving him any signs. *Ah, but wait for the concert, she will send me a sign then when I knock her off her feet.* He couldn't wait for the concert to happen and had been practising diligently each day. The day of the concert arrived, and he was eager to get home after college to spruce himself up. First he made a quick visit to the barbers to get his hair cut, and then rushed home to shower and pick out his best clothes. He opted for the green and black, check shirt that he had bought recently and was saving for this occasion, and faded, black, fitted jeans teamed with his converse shoes. He sprayed on his Hugo Boss aftershave and looked at his reflection in the mirror.

Yep, I'm ready for you Georgia. Ready to impress. He cycled up to the college and found his classmates. The canteen looked so different now with the stage set up and chairs in rows to accommodate the visitors. The stage lights were on and there was a buzz in the air. People were beginning to drift in and take their seats. The show was due to start at 8 pm. He didn't look around to see if Georgia was there, he couldn't yet. His nerves were taking over. *Stay cool. You've got this.*

A short while later one of his classmates Rob called out to Alfie to get ready to go on stage. He composed himself, put his game face on and took to the stage. He was ready to sing his song, and his classmates started to play the instrumental. He scanned the crowd super-fast, left and right.

No sign of Georgia. Where is she? He scanned again. *No, she is definitely not here. She's going to miss my song; I can't believe this. For Christ sake, none of this means anything if she doesn't show up.* He was singing now going through the motions completely deflated. *She's just running late, she'll be here*, he consoled himself. He felt that there was still time for her to see his upcoming sax performance, as he wasn't due to play that until close to the end at 10. The time whittled away, with Alfie now on a break until his next upcoming song. He stood by the stage close to the audience and subtly watched the door, hopefully waiting for Georgia to arrive. The later it got, the more anxious he became and the more fed up he felt. Once again he was called onto the stage for his saxophone solo. He played the song and felt nothing but an empty pit in his stomach as he played it.

There goes that then, he grumbled inside. *She never showed*. He just couldn't believe it. *She had seemed so keen on the idea of coming a few weeks ago, and all the students knew this show was happening in the college. Had she forgotten? No, she couldn't have. He had only seen her earlier that day in the smoking area. She just doesn't care, and never cared. Why did I ever bother? Did I honestly think I could have her?* Just then, his teacher Ross approached, interrupting his thoughts.

'What's up Alfie? You look bummed out? Aren't you happy with the show?'

'Em, no Ross. Can you keep a secret?'

'Of course, I can. What is it?'

'Ok, do you know that girl Georgia?'

'Who doesn't know her Alfie, she's a weapon. What about her?'

'She said she would come tonight and she never did. I've been preparing for weeks, got my haircut, went the whole nine yards,' confided Alfie.

'Oh, so you fancy her? Oh kid, I'm sorry about that. That was shitty, damn! Have you got it bad for her?

'After tonight, I don't know. I'm too fed up now and I can't even think,' he said, deflated.

'Come for a drink with us, come on and celebrate the night. It'll be great craic. She probably forgot Alfie or maybe something came up,' said Ross, reassuringly, recognising the look of complete disappointment on Alfie's face.

'Yeah, maybe. Look, I don't want to bring the mood down. I'm going to go home and sleep it off. Tomorrow is another day. Thanks Ross, you're a mate,' replied Alfie, in a low, defeated voice.

'Ok then buddy, remember what I said. Probably just a mix up.'

'Yeah, maybe,' said Alfie, shrugging and offering a touch of a smile to Ross, while grabbing his instrument.

He took off on his bike with his saxophone on his back, ready for home. As he cycled down the hill he noticed it was a dark, starry, night with a light soothing breeze, a sublime night, but it only served as a tease to Alfie reminding him as to the night it could have been. The night he had hoped for. Alfie woke to the sun streaming through the gap in his curtains and the sound of the birds singing. He was still very disappointed, but it was a little less raw now.

While in class anticipating the upcoming break time, he found himself very curious as to what Georgia would say about not turning up to the concert. Now this he had to hear. Eleven o' clock arrived, and he walked out to the smoking area, and saw Georgia engaged in her usual routine of chatting and smoking, while drinking her coffee.

'Hey Alfie, what's the craic?' said Georgia, perkily.

'Ah, nothing major. Same old, same old.'

He wasn't giving her much today. Maybe he was just having a bad day. She noticed he seemed noticeably quiet, and today there was no sparkle in his eyes or even a hint of a smile.

He looked quite serious. Hmm, still sexy, even when he is moody,' she giggled in her head.

'Hey Alfie, you were awesome last night,' commented Mark, one of the students from Georgia's class.

'Cheers, Mark.'

'What's this?' probed Georgia.

'The concert was last night, and Alfie was in it.'

Georgia turned to look directly at Alfie.

'Oh, sugar, was that last night? I forgot about that,' said Georgia.

'It's grand,' said Alfie, through gritted teeth.

'What did you do for the night?' said Alfie, in disbelief that she was being so nonchalant.

'Me? I just had a chilled-out night in my pyjamas watching some crappy series on Netflix. Your night was a lot more exciting by the sounds of it Alfie.'

Chilled out in her pyjamas? Alfie said out loudly in his head. *You have to be kidding me.* He couldn't fathom it. He was too disgusted to continue the conversation.

'Yeah, sure t'was alright. I must head back. Catch you later.'

Georgia felt a mood in the air, but quickly dismissed it and got back to her chat with the other lads, completely oblivious to the destruction she had caused Alfie. Blissfully unaware that he was gutted that she had not come to the concert. Much as she always prided herself on being super intuitive with people she was prone to the odd lapse in judgment.

7

Second chances

It took alfie a few days to get over his disappointment, but he managed to overcome it. It was Friday and he was on his way to guitar practice. As he was about to enter the canteen, he heard crying. He paused instantly, not knowing whether or not he should enter.

Obviously somebody in there is very upset. He listened closer and heard a woman crying, and then heard Georgia's voice consoling her. He peeped around the door frame, and found a spot where he could see her, but she couldn't see him. He watched Georgia hugging another student, a girl he didn't recognise. Her face looked sympathetic and her eyes were soft and kind. He hadn't seen her in this light before. He gathered from the conversation that this lady's dog had just died, and she was explaining to Georgia that she would never love a pet again and that her heart was broken. He listened to Georgia tell the lady that she herself, had experienced this feeling before when she lost her beloved cat. His name was Tux and he had meant so much to her. He had wandered into her backyard at a period in her life where she had been very much alone; both within herself and in terms of her relationships with others. She had held him close, confiding her deepest secrets and dreams, things she never felt safe enough to share with a human companion. Losing him felt like losing a part of herself, yet nobody in her world would be able to understand the depth of her loss and so she hadn't even attempted to explain it. Now was not the time either, she needed to focus on being that kind for someone else. Her vet had told her not to let her broken heart prevent her from giving more animals a home. There were too many out there in need and if everybody gave up, they would suffer.

'I know it's so difficult now Aoife, but think about the fantastic life you gave your dog, Max. He had a dream life, and your souls will forever be connected. He will be waiting for you when your day comes, wagging his tail and jumping into your arms. What is time Aoife? Maybe fifty years for you is actually minutes for Max who will be waiting for you. We have no idea how time travels on the other side. I know the time isn't right for you to love another pet yet Aoife and you have to heal. Believe me, I've had my heart broken continually over the years by animals but I say I can take another hit for you, I'll take a million hits, because I have all this love to give and I'm going to give it.'

Aoife's face softened and she stopped crying.

'Thank you Georgia, nobody else would understand. I live on my own and my dog was my best friend. I have no family and he was my life. I knew you would get it. You never judge.'

'Oh, I judge Aoife, but I judge those who are cruel, not kind, and you my love are a sunflower. Be kind to yourself. Leave college early and go home and do whatever you have to do. I'll cover for you with Lewis. It will get better with time, I promise you.'

They hugged and Georgia headed out for a cigarette. Alfie breezed into the canteen as if he had heard nothing and went on to find his practice room. Two hours later it was time for tea break, and he was looking forward to seeing Georgia again. He loved this side of her which he never knew existed. It was so deep and insightful. There was so much he wanted to learn about her, and he decided that everybody can forget sometimes, and it was time to forgive her for not turning up at the concert. Sure enough tea break arrived, and Alfie made his way to the smoking area.

He approached Georgia without delay.

'Georgia, you'll think I'm a nosy fecker, but I stumbled across you and that girl who was upset earlier and overheard your chat. I was on my way to practice and I wasn't sure whether to go in or not.'

'Ah, that's grand. The poor thing, her dog just died.'

'You were so kind to her, that really was so sweet. You're a great listener and you have a lovely way with words, do you know that?'

'Aw, how lovely of you Alfie. I just can't bear to see anyone sad. I'm a fixer.'

'A fixer?'

'Yeah, I see a problem and I run to fix it. I can't help myself. I'm always trying to find a solution. My brother kills me for it.'

'But isn't that a good thing?'

'Ah you know, he tells me sometimes you should try not to fix it, but just let people feel someone is listening and let them have their rant. I'm still honing my skills.'

'It looks to me like they are well-honed already.'

'You're a darling Alfie,' replied Georgia, fondly.

He felt his ears redden and a feeling of heat develop around his neck.

I'm a darling. He looked into her eyes at that moment, those far away, piercing eyes, and he noticed how they were focused on him only. He had all her attention. Her smile was fully extended but her lips were closed. A song ran into his mind, 'There She Goes' by Sixpence None the Richer.' *Where did that come from?*

'Once I had a dog who died. He was my best bud. I called him Brian. I'm not ashamed to tell you that I cried like a little girl when he passed.'

'First of all Alfie, that name is awesome. Brian. Ha! You're a scream you are, and secondly,' she whispered with empathy, 'I'm really sorry Alfie. You're warming my heart with that now. I always love a guy who has a heart for animals. It's most endearing,' said Georgia, flirtatiously. With that, she touched him on the arm with a sympathetic look. 'He was one lucky dog I'd say.'

Alfie felt like a bolt of electricity ran through his arm. It was the first time they had touched. He felt her energy run through him and it felt healing and exciting all at the same time. He felt his neck get hotter and a pressure rise through his body.

There and then, he would have given anything to just cradle her face in his hands and kiss her wildly, but hey this was real life. There were rules. Georgia realised at this moment that she had given Alfie enough now. Her father's words echoed through her mind.

Only give him the bare amount and he will be yours, 'she remembered. She took a step back.

'Oh, Alfie, is that the time? I've to get my skates on. I have vocal practice in a minute and I just realised everybody has gone back to class. It was really nice chatting to you. I'll see you later Mister.'

'Yeah, it was great, good luck with vocals, not that you'll need it. I've heard you sing. You will be the one teaching the lesson I'd say,' laughed Alfie, flirting outrageously.

'Smooth' she replied with a cheeky smile, then with her head held high and gazing upwards she chirped, 'Romeo, Romeo, where art thou Romeo,' as she made her way through the door. She could hear him laughing warmly behind her.

Yes, you bring it on and I'll be at the ready. Like a game of tennis. He made her feel warm, fuzzy, and alive. Nonetheless, she was an alpha female, and this cheeky chappy would have to be the one who was left wanting, not her. *I'll show you how long I can draw this out, I could keep it up for years and keep you guessing.*

Life had hardened her a bit, and various men excluding Jesse on her journey in life had used her, cheated on her, lied to her, and she felt she had to shield herself from hurt, and keep that barrier up at all costs.

Sometimes she felt it was hard to even relate to the young, innocent, naive girl she once was. It was as if she had dreamed up that person, she was so far away from that girl now. At times it even made her feel a little sad that she had to let that girl go, as if they had walked together on a beach, and she had all of a sudden let go of that little girl's hand, and left her behind, abandoned her. She would then reassure herself that she did the right thing. That naive girl got stomped on. This new version was getting by a lot better in the world, and she would have to stay.

Georgia always had a very artistic way of looking at herself and the world around her. She worked very hard at keeping that hidden, because she had observed the rules and etiquette of society for long enough to know there was a time and place.

Monday morning dawned, and Georgia was making sure to examine her wardrobe and take a little extra time getting ready. She wanted to look damn good for Alfie and make him drool.

Let me draw you into my spider's web, she playfully laughed to herself, while fantasising about him. Later that morning, her teacher, Lewis informed the class that the students downstairs were having a lunchtime concert.

'Oh yes! A break from class. A little doss time,' she whispered to Ben, her buddy.

'Yeah, bring it on. We're sitting together Missy,' said Ben, excitedly.

'Why of course, would we have it any other way?'

She loved to be playful with the guys, even her male friends, and always enjoyed every opportunity to chase a laugh. She skipped down the stairs with Ben and the rest of the class, and there was Alfie on the stage holding a cello.

Jesus, he plays the Cello too, Wow. She took her seat beside Ben and looked right up at Alfie, who was getting set to play. She had chosen a seat at the front where she could smile playfully up at him. The look that says I notice you right now, and I'm impressed, very impressed. Alfie immediately noticed her and affectionately returned her gaze. As he stared right into her eyes from the stage, his mouth was closed and still, like he was concentrating on his music but aware of her.

I see you my beauty, I hope you know how much I want you right now. He reckoned he was getting a sign from her.

She hadn't taken her eyes off him the entire time, but then everybody's eyes were on him, he figured. *Maybe she was just enjoying the music.*

Alfie went on to finish his performance and various students approached him to tell him how much they enjoyed it, but he only wanted to hear it from her. After a few minutes Georgia went up to him.

'Wow, check you out Mister, that was divine to listen to. I never knew you played the Cello. I'm blown away right now and I'm uber impressed!

At this moment he felt a little overcome with nerves, so he sat on the edge of the stage to steady himself.

'Are you ok, Alfie? You look a bit pale,' said Georgia, in a concerned tone, while leaning over him, putting her hand on his shoulder. As she bent over him, her long blonde hair rested on his chest.

Oh Jesus, her hair in on my chest right now, I can't cope, thought Alfie, frayed with nerves at this moment of closeness. He could smell her perfume and it had a lovely strawberry scent that he instantly adored. He felt her scent was magnetic and his lips slightly parted as he inhaled her sneakily.

'Yeah, I'm fine thanks, I'm just nursing a hangover today,' he lied.

'Phew, thank God that's all it is. I was worried about you for a moment and I'm glad you are alright,' she said, straightening herself up again.

Ross, the teacher then called out for everyone to take their seats, as the concert was resuming.

'I had better get back to my seat or I'll be in trouble', she said, sarcastically. 'Before I go, I must say, I'm very sorry that I missed that concert of yours lately. A big failure on my part. I'll have to start paying more attention around here,' said Georgia, with a glint in her eye.

'Oh, well, thank you. Let me put it this way, your absence was noticed,' said Alfie, cheekily.

'Oh, was it now?' she grinned back. 'Best news I heard all day.'

As she walked away she glanced back at him over her shoulder, letting him know she was interested.

A sign? I just got it. It's like Christmas day, he daydreamed. The following day as usual, he was excited at the thought of seeing Georgia again, but this time when he went into the smoking area there was no sign of her. She was always there before him, so this was unusual. He felt perplexed and assumed perhaps her class was working overtime. Break-time came and went, and Georgia never came.

Hmm, has she given up smoking? Or is she sick and not in today? Where is she? He was disappointed, especially since she had signalled her interest just yesterday. He was hoping to extend that flirtation just another bit. He headed back to class and over the next two days she was still missing. He longed to ask the guys out in the smoking area if they knew where she was, but he knew they were no fools, and would smell a rat, and know he was interested in Georgia. He didn't want the guys messing anything up for him, so he just pretended everything was normal.

Inside he felt like he had got a snapshot of what life in the college would be without her. It felt empty and flat and somewhat meaningless. He spent those days fearing that she might possibly have left the course, and he missed her, ALOT.

Friday beckoned and as he entered the smoking area

once again, hoping to see her, he was granted his wish. She was standing in her usual spot, with her hair in loose curls, wearing a white, knitted, polo-neck jumper, black leggings and faux, brown Ugg boots. He noticed the soles of her boots were so worn down, that she might as well have been walking on her bare feet. He loved her devil may-care-attitude. She wasn't wearing any make up either and that appealed to him all the more.

She's back, thank God.

'Hi Bee,' he said, walking up beside her.

'Bee, who's that Alfie? Did somebody change my name and not tell me?'

'Yeah, I did, while you were away. Bee for bright eyes, that's your new name now. You always look like you've had twenty hours sleep,' he laughed.

'Do I? Jeez, I'm flattered. Do you want to make me blush? Because it's working,' she said coyly, slightly blushing and looking down at her feet momentarily. 'Now tell me, how do I spell that, is it Be or Bee? Which do we like better?' she cheekily asked, trying to fumble for anything, as he had caught her off-guard. Alfie laughed as he found her entertaining as always.

'I think we will go with B-e-e, sounds better.'

'And do I get a say in any of this?' asked Georgia, in a flirty tone.

'No actually, you don't.'

Georgia felt a flutter, instantly attracted to the fact that Alfie had taken charge and had given her this lovely compliment.

'Anyway, I thought you had left us Bee.'

'Now as if I could do that Alfie, I'd want to be crazy.

72

Actually, I was in Italy with my sister, niece and nephew for a few days.'

So that's where she was, he mused, reassured at the very thought of it.

'Really, wow! I'm delighted for you. Did you have a nice time?'

'Oh, I had a wicked time, thanks for asking. I always wanted to go there.'

She proceeded to tell him about some of the sites they visited and the fun they had, and just as they were wrapping up their chat, he couldn't help but be more forward with her as he was on a roll today.

'And tell me, did you meet any nice Italian man who swept you off your feet?' inquired Alfie, expecting her to say no.

'Strangely enough, I actually did, he is coming over to see me next weekend.'

Alfie's face dropped and his mouth opened wide. He looked stumped and couldn't believe his ears.

'Really, are you actually serious Bee?' he asked, looking like his dog had just been run over.

'Eh, no, I'm not being serious. I was just messing with you. I have more of a penchant for Irish guys as it happens.'

'Ooh aren't you a right madam? You had me worried there for a moment,' stammered Alfie, looking all relieved.

'Ha, that's nothing compared to what I can do to you,' she replied, laughing and edging for the door. 'See you around Mister,' said Georgia, smiling as she breezed out of view. Alfie stood there grinning, watching her the entire time.

Hmm, heart breaker alert. He wasn't used to girls being this cool with him.

Over the weekend, Alfie found it hard to think of anything other than Georgia. He felt like he had become closer to her the previous week, and she kept running through his mind. He was due to meet his pals for drinks on the Saturday night but spent the night distracted. His friends, Tom and Peter noticed he was quieter than usual.

'What's going on with you man?' asked Tom, as he studied Alfie.

'What do you mean? I'm grand.'

'You seem a little distracted. Has somebody got a woman on his mind?' inquired Tom.

'Em, no,' replied Alfie, looking a bit rattled.

'I'm not convinced, are you Pete?' laughed Tom.

'I think you're right Tom, somebody has gotten under Alfie's skin, and we want to know who it is,' cheered on Peter.

'Alright, alright, there's a girl, you happy now?' said Alfie, somewhat impatiently, but also slightly humoured.

'Spill buddy. We want all the gory details. Who is she? said Peter.

'Ah, she goes to the music course but she's not in my class.'

'And…. What does she look like? What's her name?' asked Peter.

'It's Georgia and don't laugh now, but she is as pretty as Princess Grace.'

'Princess Grace, Jesus kid, you sound like someone in love,' laughed Pete, with Tom exploding into laughter at the same time.

'We need to see her photo pronto,' said Tom eagerly, while sipping away on his pint.

'If ye stop badgering me, I'll get one.'

'Sweet, looking forward to that,' said Pete.

Alfie wondered how he would actually make this possible. He began to feel glad that his friends had pushed him, because he realised he needed a photo of her on his phone anyway, for himself, so he could look at it and dream about her when he wasn't at the college.

I must create an opportunity,' he plotted. The following week at the college he noticed Georgia's class were practising. They seemed to be rehearsing for the summer programme. He walked into the canteen pretending he was on his way somewhere with his saxophone and looked up at the stage. There she stood among the rest of her class singing 'Don't Stop Believing' by Journey. She was wearing a frilly blouse and her skinny, blue jeans emphasised her curves. A few students strolled in to hear the practice session, and Alfie decided he could blend in with them and take a peep also, without looking too obvious. He saw a guy whip out his camera phone and start recording.

This is the moment you can record her and pretend you are just recording the group singing their song. He casually took out his phone and with a big smile, began to record the group. *Result!! I can show this to the lads,* delighted that he had got the opportunity. Recording done, he headed towards the door next to the stage, but not without first casting a glance at her direction. He gazed up at her, with a silly grin that he wasn't even aware of, and waited for her to return his glance. She was singing her song, pretending not to notice him, so he had no choice but to keep walking without any acknowledgement.

She's a tough nut to crack. He was feeling frustrated she hadn't noticed him. He just wanted a moment, just her and him, but he had been denied the pleasure. Luckily, he had the footage though. *I've got gold right here. I can look at her all day now*, he dreamily thought to himself. That evening Alfie was at home waiting for his friends Tom and Peter to arrive back from work. These three aswell as being flatmates were also good friends. He was in the middle of cooking dinner when they arrived and crashed onto the couch after their long day at work. Tom was a barman, and Peter an I.T. Technician.

'Hey guys, remember I said I'd get ye a photo of Georgia?' said Alfie.

'Yeah, did you get it?' they both asked enthusiastically.

'I did better than that, I got a video of her,' said Alfie, excitedly.

'Sweet Lord, hand it over,' said Peter.

Alfie proudly handed his phone over to them, and with keen interest they watched her and the group sing the song.

'You weren't kidding Alfie. She's a sexy bitch,' insisted Tom, with Peter nodding.

'Hey, mind your manners. That might be my future wife you are talking about,' interrupted Alfie, in a parental type tone.

'Future wife, whoa, you have never said that about any woman mate,' said Tom.

'I know but this girl is different. She has got under my skin,' explained Alfie, throwing himself onto the couch.

'I'm shocked. Are you in love man?' probed Peter, looking stunned.

'I dunno, I might be, but only recently she broke up

with her boyfriend of six years. She probably isn't in a rush to be all serious with a guy so soon again, don't ya think?'

'Hmmm, I suppose the important question here is does she seem really interested in you too?' said Tom.

'It's hard to tell, she is sending me mixed signals at the moment. I mean, sometimes I think I see passion in her eyes, and other times it's like I don't exist. Hot and cold, you know?'

'Just be careful, my man. You don't need a woman wrecking your head now do you? Just play it cool. She is absolutely gorgeous though, and I'd throw you under a bus to have her for myself,' laughed Peter.

'Hands off mate, she's mine. Ye are never going to meet her now,' laughed Alfie.

'I'm with Peter on this one, I'd throw ye both under a bus. She is what I'd call a global beauty,' said Tom.

'What's a global beauty?' asked Alfie.

'It means, guys all over the world would fancy her, no matter what their nationality,' explained Tom.

Just then, another song ran into Alfie's mind, 'When You're In Love With A Beautiful Woman' by Dr. Hook & The Medicine Woman.'

'Song worm,' laughed Alfie.

'Oh no, I hate those, what is it?' asked Tom.

'When you're in love with a beautiful woman,' said Alfie.

With that, the three of them broke into laughter at the same time.

'Come on, throw something on Netflix there, and forget about her for the night,' said Peter.

'Yeah, you're right, my head needs a break. It's turning to mush,' said Alfie.

8

'Float like a butterfly, sting like a bee'

The following morning Alfie left the house bright and early. He jumped on his bike and as he was making his way up the hill to the college, he crossed the bridge and saw Georgia. This was the first time he had seen her on her way to college. They usually just met up at breaktime.

Feck, she must be living nearby. I need to catch up with her, and we can walk up the hill together. For once, I can have her all to myself without the guys being in the way. He slowed down and observed her, as she was still a good 20 metres ahead of him and hadn't yet seen him. Her hair was piled high on top of her head in an unusual style, and it reminded him of a medieval hairstyle. She was wearing a blue knitted top with white jeans. Her over-the-shoulder brown bag was swinging in the wind as she walked, and her black headphones hugged her ears comfortably. She was completely unaware of the admiring stares of the men who passed her in the street, and she appeared to be lost in thought looking content on her way to the college.

There's my girl. She doesn't know it yet, but she will. He pulled his bike into the side of the road for a moment to let the traffic pass. He ran his fingers through his hair and checked his clothes. He was wearing his favourite grandfather top with dark blue jeans, and his trusted comfortable converse shoes. He realised that he was making a lot more effort with his appearance these days. Contented with how he looked, he headed for the hill. His heart began to beat faster with anticipation as he approached her. She was still ahead of him and walking relatively fast, but he managed to catch up with her halfway up the hill, walking his bike as he went.

He reached out and touched her arm gently to get her attention because he knew she had headphones on, and she jumped at his touch.

'Jeez, you gave me a fright Alfie, I was completely away in my own world. I feel silly getting so startled,' said Georgia, sounding a little out of breath and her face first defensive and then relieved.

She tugged at her headphones to remove them and swiped off the music on her phone.

'Damn, I didn't mean to frighten you this early in the morning, sorry Bee. I didn't know I looked so scary.'

Georgia laughed out loudly in response and lifted her sunglasses to sit on her head.

'I'm a big eejit as you can see, I can get a little defensive. I must think I'm going to be attacked at any time,' she joked.

'Aw, you're sweet Bee, sure who would attack you?'

'You'd be surprised.'

Had she been attacked before? Alfie wondered.

'Let's start again, good morning Mister.'

'Yeah good morning Bee, I haven't seen you around here before. Do you live nearby?'

'Yeah, I live at the bottom of the hill by the funeral home and the river.'

'And tell me, do you live in the funeral home or the river, which is it?

'Hahaha stop it you, it's too early in the morning,' laughed Georgia, realising she had described where she lived in a bit of an odd way.

'So anyway, are you enjoying the course? What did you do before starting at the Abbey?'

'Watashi wa nihongo o benkyo shite imashita,' Georgia replied, speaking Japanese.

'What the hell was that?' he inquired, looking shocked. 'Was that Japanese?' asked Alfie, wide-eyed with interest.

'Haha, yes, it means I was studying Japanese.'

'Oh my God, talk about bringing a man to his knees. Jeez, you have some tricks up your sleeve,' he giggled. 'You speak it so fluently, how long were you studying it- twenty years?'

'No, actually, just a few months.'

'A few months, and you speak that well. Say something else in Japanese.'

'Anata wa watashi o warawaseru,' said Georgia, in her best Japanese accent.

'Such a divine language, what did that mean? Were you just abusing me?' joked Alfie.

'No, I was saying you make me laugh.'

'How do you say you are beautiful in Japanese then?' asked Alfie, ready to take advantage of an opportunity to flirt some more.

'Anata wa utsukushidesu.'

'Anata wa utsuk, ah, I forget the rest.'

'Anata mo ne,' said Georgia, smiling away.

'And that meant?'

'You'll just have to go look it up, won't you?'

80

Alfie took out his phone and asked her to spell it so he could look it up, and she did.

'It probably means you're a big eejit I'd say.'

'I'm sure you'll work it out.'

It meant 'And you too'.

'Where did you do the course? Tell me everything you interesting alien you.'

'I went to University, but I hated my teacher, so I left after a few months. I gave it a lot of thought first though, because I loved it and it came very easy to me.'

'Yeah, I can see that. Oh, that's a shame,' said Alfie, looking slightly disappointed for her. 'But, it's probably a good thing for us at the college, otherwise you wouldn't be there.'

'True.'

They continued to chat all the way up the hill exchanging questions about courses they had done, and then it was time for them both to cross the road to the college. Georgia hesitated and looked a little nervous and uptight. There were cars coming, but they were quite a distance away, and Alfie noticed her looking unsure.

'You're grand, those cars are way back. Are you nervous crossing the road?' asked Alfie surprised, as he was so used to seeing everybody jaywalk.

'Yeah, I got knocked down years ago, and I feel a bit weird about it. Just take no notice of me, I'm building up to it,' explained Georgia, looking embarrassed and unsure.

Alfie reached out his hand to her, 'Take my hand, I got you. Trust me.'

'Thank you, what a gentleman,' said Georgia, with a serene smile adorning her face.

They crossed the road hand in hand.

In that moment he held her hand tightly and reassuringly in a very manly, protective way. It was a glimmer of what he could have with her if she was his girlfriend, and he didn't want to let go. In fact, he didn't want to go to the Abbey now. He wanted to keep holding her hand, take the day off, and have the best day ever walking anywhere with her and finding out more and more about her.

He felt her hand wrapped up in his was cold, soft and gentle. He liked that her face looked assured and happy, but when they got across the road she slowly slipped her hand out from his grip.

'Thanks, that was kind. You're kind,' said Georgia, appreciating the gesture.

That was so sweet. Not bad at all for a cheeky chappy.

'Where did you get knocked down you poor thing?'

'In Paris on a romantic getaway weekend with an ex of mine.'

She felt her usual confident act slip and started to feel nervous and shy after the intimate moment she had shared with Alfie.

'Paris, woah, that's not something you hear every day. What happened exactly?'

'Oh, I might tell you another day. We're almost at the door.'

'Cool.'

He noticed Georgia looked nervous, and he hadn't seen her like that before. He was observing a different layer of her, a shy layer. Her face was a little flushed and she looked a bit flustered. He was trying to catch her eye as they talked, but she wasn't using her usual confident eye contact and looked away most of the time.

Am I making her nervous? Does she like me? She is acting shy around me and it's so cute. She's cute.

'Anyway, I gotta run, I'm going to be late. Catch you later,' said Georgia.

'Yeah, see you at small break.'

With that, she swiftly climbed the stairs to her classroom, and Alfie went to his class downstairs and took his seat in the front section. He felt like he was in a cloud, and played back the last fifteen minutes in his head over and over.

I got to walk with her today, just me and her, like we were boyfriend and girlfriend. I held her hand, I found out she speaks Japanese, and she was knocked down. She's so interesting. I feel there's an ocean of stuff to find out about her, but she gets cagey. I must mind my pace with her. Take it easy, slowly. She is like a butterfly, lands on your shoulder but never stays for long, always leaving when you want her to stay.

Georgia was now back at class and trying hard to concentrate on the lesson. She had been thinking lately of becoming a piano teacher in the future, but Alfie kept trickling through her mind. She was feeling quite taken with him after their walk to the college, and was feeling butterflies in her stomach like a beautiful ache. When she played back the part where they had held hands crossing the road, she wondered if he was just a player. He seemed so confident, witty, and charming.

He is probably like this with all women. What makes me special? She had met charming guys in the past, a little like him, and they had turned out to be toads, so how could she trust him? *How old is he?* She was thirty-two but presumed he might be only twenty-four. She was *far* too old for him. She figured he was probably passing the time flirting with her, and she warned herself to stay guarded, but she did want to know his age. She would have to grill him about that at tea break. She was taking a closer look at him now in her mind, as he had caught her attention on that walk. Two hours later, tea break arrived, and she breezed down the stairs in her usual fashion, grabbed her coffee and headed outside. Ben was leaning against the wall and she joined him for a chat. Five minutes later Alfie appeared.

'What's the craic Alfie?' said Ben.

'Ah, nothing much Ben. I've just been knee-deep in music intervals for the morning,' said Alfie, in an exasperated tone. 'Boring really.'

'Yeah, it sounds boring. I was just showing Georgia a picture of me when I was young and handsome,' exclaimed Ben to Alfie.

'You're still handsome,' said Georgia, in her charming fashion.

'Give us a look. You were like a blonde, surfer dude,' said Alfie.

'Haha, was I? Yeah, a surfer that didn't surf. You'll get to my age one day too.'

'What age is that?'

'Forty-seven and I feel like a vintage car mate.'

'What age are you Alfie? Twenty-one?'

'Ha, I wish, I'm thirty-one. I'll be thirty-two next February on Valentine's Day,' said Alfie, with a smile.

'Thirty-one? I thought you were twenty-four. You look so young. You are only a year younger than me,' disclosed Georgia. 'And my birthday is on Valentine's Day too. I thought I was the only one born on that day haha.'

'Really? We share the same birthday. How cool is that?'

Just at that moment, he remembered his mother.

84

9

When the boy becomes a man

She had always called him her little Valentine. She had named him Alfie, after passionately loving the original Alfie movie starring Michael Caine. His mother Isabella was a real romantic, and always loved the cheeky chappy type. She told Alfie how she had found his name when he was little. She had even married a cheeky chappy, his father Paddy, and had gone on to have three sons Alfie, James and Martin. She adored them all but had a special connection with Alfie. He had inherited her stunning looks as she was tall with long brown luscious hair, sallow skin, brown eyes and a gentle, kind smile. His father was a good-looking man, 6 ft tall with black hair, blue eyes, clean-shaven skin and with a glint in his eye. This left women smouldering for him but he had chosen Isabella, because to him, she was not only beautiful but highly intelligent, a wonderful listener, and kind to all. Sometimes she was too kind, at-tracting needy types. She was always tending to somebody, forgetting her own needs, but Paddy was more shrewd.

He was a businessman who worked in recruitment, and with his perfect wife and three sons, he felt he had it all. Alfie had always been a charming little boy making everyone laugh, singing and performing, and was prone to picking up half-dead birds and other animals, and bringing them home to care for them. He was carefree and happy, hanging out with his friends being your typical boy, playing by the river and getting up to mischief. Isabella would scold him when he returned home late, but he knew all the right words to get her on side, just like his father.

Life was picture perfect, until destiny threw him and his family the cruellest blow that would knock them all to their knees. Alfie had taken the day off school as he was feeling sick. He watched his mother potter around the kitchen doing errands and making him food, while he sat at the kitchen table reading his Beano comic. He was ten years old, and it was Thursday the 14th November, 1997, a date that was to be burned into his mind forever.

While making food his mother unexpectedly moaned loudly, clutching her heart. Alfie had felt a rush of pressure run through him and looked up at her. She stood behind the kitchen counter with a terrified look in her eyes. He knew something was wrong and ran towards her, and just as he reached out to grab her, she fell to the floor. She had suffered a massive heart attack. Alfie fell to the ground by her side.

'Mommy, mommy, I don't know what to do, tell me what to do,' cried Alfie, panicked out of his mind.

'Ring 999,' Isabella feebly answered, clutching her chest and in excruciating pain. Alfie went to get the phone which was in the hallway, and just then she grabbed his arm and looked into his eyes.

'I love you son, go now.'

'I love you too Mom, just hang on please, just hang on,' begged Alfie.

He ran for the phone in the hall completely freaked out, lifted the receiver and rang 999. He urgently blurted out his message giving them the address, desperate to get back to check on his mother in the kitchen. When he returned to the kitchen, he knew at a glance that she was dead. He threw himself on top of her, beating on her chest with his fists and crying.

'No, no, don't leave me,' but Isabella had left the earth and he knew it.

His neighbour Margot, a truly caring, country woman in her sixties heard all the commotion from her sitting room just a few doors away. As she was reading her book she was startled by the sound of an ambulance. She looked out her window, and saw it had stopped outside Alfie's house. She was upset and concerned, as she had known the Broderick's since they moved in fifteen years ago. She had lived in her home all her life, and since she was an only child, she remained there caring for her mother until she died a year ago. She had never known her father. She rushed into her neighbour's house and was horrified to see the front door open, and an ambulance crew working on Alfie's mother, who was lying on the floor in the kitchen. She scanned the room, and saw Alfie crying his heart out in a corner of the kitchen, crouched on the floor with his head in his hands.

'Oh my dear boy, what happened?' asked Margot.

'The ambulance men said she had a heart attack,' he sobbed.

Margot peered behind her and heard one of the crew.

'We've lost her. Stop the compressions.'

Margot knew instantly Isabella was dead, and she felt devastated. She turned to Alfie who had heard their words like a knife through his heart.

'Now listen to me Alfie, I know this feels like the worst day of your life, and you think the sun will never shine again for you, but hear me when I tell you, it will. I lost my own mother a year ago, and you will get through it. Your mother adored you, you were the apple of her eye. Life is a funny thing, it's beautiful and ugly, but believe me son, there are far more beautiful times than ugly ones. Everything is going to be ok. I'll ring your daddy and the boys, and we will all hold each other tightly, for days if we need to. I've got you.'

Alfie jumped into her arms, and held her tighter than he had ever held anyone before. After what seemed like an eternity crying, he paused.

'My throat is sore from crying.'

'I know sweetheart, I know,' said Margot, with sympathy bounding from her eyes.

She called his father who immediately jumped into his car and headed to the hospital. Margot brought Alfie with her in her car, collecting his younger brothers from playschool on the way, so that they could all be together as a family. His father and brothers were inconsolable at the news, and his father stayed strong for his boys. Paddy took the next few weeks off work to grieve with them, and come to terms with the cruel blow they had all been dealt. When things began to settle down Paddy took Alfie to one side.

'Alfie I know you are only ten years old, but now that your mum is gone, I'm going to need your help to look after your younger brothers.'

Martin was aged four and James was two years old.

'I'm hoping you will be my second in command and help me run this house. I know it's not fair but I have to feed you guys, and so I must go to work. Can you do it son?' asked Paddy, with a lump in his throat, full of guilt that he had to ask his son for help.

Alfie put on his bravest face and looked his father straight in the eye.

'So you mean I can boss them around? Yeah definitely,' answered Alfie, playfully, trying to add a spot of humour to cheer up his father. Seriously you and I Pops, we will run the ship from now on, don't worry.'

That day, the boy became a man, and his father watched in awe as Alfie helped get his brothers off to playschool. He made lunches, dinners, washed and cleaned, helped with their homework and tucked them into bed at night. Alfie and his father were like a tag team, and the only time Alfie got proper time for himself was when he played his guitar at home. This was the guitar his father had got him as a surprise and a thank you gift for all his hard work. As the years rolled by, Alfie missed out on the regular things a boy his age would get to do, like school disco's and hanging out with the guys, but he promised himself when his brothers would become of age he would leave and go wild for the rest of his life making it up to himself. It was his golden nugget that kept him going through all the hardship. When he was twenty years old his father sat him down.

'Now, son, I don't think I need to tell you what an angel you have been for me do I?'

'I know Dad, sure I'm brilliant,' laughed Alfie.

'The boys are older now son, and I don't need you as my second in command anymore. We did a good job didn't we? I know it wasn't as good as if Mom was here, but we had happy times, and I think we pulled it off under the circumstances.'

'We did Dad, we did,' said Alfie, with pride.

'It's time for you to spread your wings now son and fly. Forget about girls. They are too much heartache. Go to college, do the course you love, find the career you love and travel the world.'

'Yeah, and I'd like to find a nice lassie too Pop,' said Alfie, with a grin.

'They're not worth it son. You'll only get your heart broken. Look at me. Date them and leave them if you want my advice,' said Paddy, with a look of pain etched on his face.

'Don't worry Pops, I've a lot of living to make up for, and I'm going to go bloody well wild.'

'That's my boy, live it up for the two of us. But be safe, do you hear me? My heart can't take another blow, remember that.'

'I will Pops, I will,' reassured Alfie, looking his father dead in the eye.

After weeks of careful consideration and deep soul searching, during a walk to the shops, the answer became clear to Alfie.

Become a chef! He had done plenty of cooking over the years for the family, and while at first, he hated it, as time went by, he found it relaxed him and gave him a great deal of pleasure. He went on to train as a chef in a college in Galway, and after three years, as the course drew to an end the lecturer brought in career advisers. Alfie and his class were told all about the different career options available, and Alfie's ears pricked when he was exposed to the idea of working as a chef on a cruise ship.

'I'll do that,' he said enthusiastically, forgetting his composure for a brief moment.

'Super, come meet with me after the session, good lad,' said the career adviser.

After the session he was versed on all the positives and negatives of working on a cruise ship, but Alfie was convinced this would get him around the world, and he would feel free. The wheels were put in motion, and he called a family meeting at home. His father and two brothers who were now happy, well-adjusted teenagers were very curious as to why they were being summoned. They sat around the kitchen table, and Alfie stood before them looking a little nervous but excited.

'I've got a job as a chef on a cruise ship lads. I might be gone a while.'

A massive smile lit the faces of his father and brothers.

'Bloody brilliant Alfie, thrilled for you brother,' said Martin.

His Dad and James were equally enthusiastic.

'When are you leaving?' asked James.

'I leave in two days.'

'No better guy. I'm proud of you son,' said Paddy.

'Thanks so much for your blessing lads. Now, listen, if you guys ever need me, I'll be at the other end of the phone, or if you ever need me to come home, I'll be back like a blue ass fly. You know that don't ye?'

They jumped up off their chairs and hugged him tightly and formed a circle with their arms around each other.

'To the Broderick clan, Forever in Arms,' cheered his father. 'Wait, go get your mothers picture from the shelf James.'

James got the picture and handed it to his father.

'Thanks son, we will go again.'

He clutched the picture of Isabella to his chest, so that she was included in the moment.

'To the Broderick clan, Forever in Arms.'

They all held each other shoulder to shoulder in a circle, unified by their love for each other. They had a bond that could never be broken, and had their little traditions over the years that made them happy. They had always set a place at the table for Isabella, and put her picture on the table mat, so that they felt her presence as they dined. Paddy would kiss her picture every night before getting into bed. He had never dated any woman since she died. He just couldn't see how you could top perfect, so why try! He didn't want his lads to ever feel the heartbreak he felt every day, so he made it his business to protect them all he could, and warned them never to fall in love. Watching Alfie leave for the cruise made him and his sons terribly sad, but they were high with excitement that this bird could now get to fly. In their minds, Alfie, more than anyone, had earned the right to have a fantastic life, after all he had done for them over the years.

10

'I'm shipping up to Boston, whoa'

Alfie was on the road to discovery, and taking to his new job like a duck to water. He was making firm friends with his fellow chefs, and the crew. Life was never dull on the ship, because he was getting to see many east coast states of America, going from Florida to New Jersey, to New York and onto Massachusetts. He revelled in the freedom it gave him, and when he wasn't cooking, he was partying, drinking, dancing and meeting women. He figured Margot was right when she told him as a boy that the sun would shine again for him, because it was shining brightly right now. Yes, he had taken a bite out of the rotten apple as a child when his mother died, but he knew he had to go forward, and here now, he was having the time of his life. Every so often he would ring home to check on his family and was glad to be reassured they were all alright. Women on the ship were throwing themselves at him, because of his rugged good looks and his charming personality. He was very popular with both men and women, young and old. He tried however, not to let anyone get too close, and never shared his innermost feelings. All that stuff was a million miles away, back in Galway and that is where he wanted to keep it.

Throughout all the partying and the stop-overs at the different ports, he stayed true to his caring nature, and enjoyed looking after the older folk on the ship. After five years of life on the high seas, he felt it was time to go home. He was missing his family and the green fields of Galway. He felt it was time for a change, so he handed in his notice and made plans to leave.

When he arrived back in Galway, he was greeted by his father who had aged a little bit more than he expected, and his two teenage brothers who by now, had grown into two young men. James had a girlfriend Saoirse, and was working in a music store, and Martin was just finishing his first year studies at Galway University; an English Lit student, and vice president of the LGBTi+ society. Alfie was so proud of the way James had embraced his sexuality and the way he wished to help other gay, young men and women to get the supports they needed. A lot had changed while Alfie was away, and he felt lonely at the thought of it. He went back to stay with his father while he figured out his next move, and within a few weeks it scarcely felt as if he had been away at all.

He picked up some work at a local bar called O'Flaherty's. It was a traditional Irish bar with lots of Irish music and sing songs every night of the week.

'Well, would ya look who it is, if it's not Paddy's son Alfie,' said an old man, sitting at the bar, who Alfie didn't recognise. 'We thought we would never see you again.'

Alfie looked closer studying his face and then the penny dropped. It was Old Man Winters from the local newsagents, or at least that is what he and his brothers called him.

'Oh, nice to see you Sir, yeah I'm back. Home was calling, what can I say? Actually, do you remember Margot? She was an elderly lady who lived next to my family.'

'I do of course son, sure she is still pottering around,' said Old Man Winters.

'Great, I have to pay her a visit. She was very good to us as kids, always checking in on us.'

'A fine woman she is indeed. You need to join us for a sing song some night.'

'God, I don't know. I haven't taken out my guitar in years.'

'Well, get practising young fella, we need some fresh blood around here and the lassies will love you.'

'Maybe I will.'

The seed had been planted, and all thanks to the old man.

On his nights off, Alfie would plonk himself down on the couch in his father's house next to the fire, and try to reignite his guitar skills. It kept him busy and made him feel peace and joy. After a few weeks he decided to go along to the Friday night sing song, and bravely brought along his guitar. It was a bit of a challenge as he only sang in front of his family up to this. He got himself a pint and sat down with a mixed group of young and old, fifteen in total, and when it came time for him to sing, he blasted out one of his favourite Shane McGowan songs, 'Dirty Old Town.' The other singers and drinkers at the bar looked gobsmacked as he sang. The passion out of this young man was palpable.

'Some voice you have there lad, you need to do something with that. All that passion has to go somewhere,' said one of the guys at the bar.

He was delighted he had joined them, and had an epic night playing his guitar and singing. The women at the bar were throwing eyes at each other, as if to say, who is he?

'He is absolutely gorgeous,' said Mary at the bar. 'If only I was ten years younger.'

'Ten years, try thirty Mary,' said Brid, another woman at the Bar. 'You are in your fifties for God's sake.'

Alfie was the star of the show, and they all let him know it. He had a delightful way about him, humble and kind, no traces of his ego, and he always knew what to say. He carried on working at the bar for the next year and a half, happy as could be, and glad he had come back from the cruise. He knew all of this was temporary, because he was ambitious and had dreams, he just didn't know what they were yet. On a fun sing song night at the bar, a Cork man approached him.

'Hi, Alfie is it?'

'Yeah, that's me, do I know you?' asked Alfie, a little bewildered.

'Haha, no, you don't but I'm a music teacher from Cork. You can probably tell by the accent?'

'Yeah, I can. It's a great accent though in fairness.'

'I just wanted to tell you I was really impressed with your singing and your guitar playing, and these people are stone mad about you.'

'Thank you very much. That's very good of you,' answered Alfie, humbly.

'We run music courses in Cork. My name is Ross by the way, I forgot to mention that. If you are ever interested in a place give me a shout. I'll give you my number.'

'Pleased to meet you Ross. I won't lie, it sounds very interesting. I'm really into music lately. Thanks so much.

Are you up in Galway for the night?'

'I'm here on holidays with the wife. I really enjoyed you, and one of the guys told me you were a barman here, so take my number and have a think.'

'I most definitely will, thanks Ross. I'll have a good think about it, so I will.'

Ross handed him the phone number, and Alfie was wondering if this was signpost as to what he should do next. He went home and talked to his father about it. It was a bit of a deal moving to Cork, but it sounded like a really good idea, and he was finding music fulfilling lately.

'What does your heart tell you to do?' asked his father, upon being told Alfie's news.

'It says to jump Pops.'

'Then jump son, think of it like a new adventure. Sure you were never going to stay working in the bar forever now were you?'

'You're right, I wasn't. Thanks Pops. Will you and the lads be ok?' asked Alfie, feeling a little bit guilty about leaving again.

'Sure didn't we manage while you were away before? Ring that man and get a place on that course.'

'I'll do it now,' said Alfie, and his face lit up with excitement.

Cork here I come, but not before visiting Margot. He had been so busy that he realised he had forgotten to call on her since coming home. He felt bad about it. She was important to him, and he had things to say to her. On his way back to his father's house he stopped at her gate. The front garden looked overgrown, and the paint was peeling off the house. He knocked on the door and saw the curtain twitch. Margot answered the door, full of glee at the sight of Alfie, and wrapped her arms around him.

'Come in, come in, my handsome boy,' she said, enthusiastically.

'Thank you Margot, it's wonderful to see you. I'm scolding myself for taking this long to visit you,' said Alfie, looking slightly ashamed.

'Never mind that Alfie, let me take a look at you.'

She raised her head to study his face as she was only 5ft tall and Alfie was 5ft 11". She peered into his big, brown, mischievous eyes, noticing his sallow skin and his cheeky smile. He had a bum fluff beard as she called it, and his brown hair was rugged and in need of a haircut.

'You look handsome boy, you always did. Come sit down in the lounge and tell me about your travels.'

'Let me make you a cuppa first Margot,' said Alfie, heading for the kitchen.

'I'd love that, sweet boy you are.'

Alfie made them both a cup of tea, and sat down in the flowery armchair next to her and told her all about his experiences on the cruise ship. He also told her of his upcoming plans to go to Cork to study music.

'It's all wonderful my love, but something is missing,' said Margot, concerned.

'What's that?' asked Alfie, curious to hear her pearls of wisdom.

'You haven't mentioned that you have the love of a good woman. I know you mentioned seeing girls on the ship for a while, but what about love?'

'Ah no, I'm not looking for that. I haven't met anybody to convince me either.'

'Is it ever because you have closed your heart to the idea?' inquired Margot, investigating further.

'Truthfully, I agree with Pops when he tells me to stay away from all that stuff,' said Alfie, shrugging.

'But Alfie, your father is coming from a place of pain and hurt after what happened to your wonderful Mother. I totally understand why he feels the way he does, but everybody has a story, and that is his story, not yours.'

'I never thought about it that way,' responded Alfie, surprised at her words.

'I suppose what I'm trying to tell you Alfie is that once upon a time I knew love. I was close to the same age as you are now. I was twenty-eight when I met a man, and I truly fell in love with him. We were together for five years, and making plans for the future, but then he got cancer and died three months later. It absolutely broke me. I remember going to the seaside the day he died, and I found a spot where it was totally quiet and isolated. I threw my fists up to the sky and roared up to God about the unfairness of it all. It was a tough time, but I got through it, but do you know what? Those five years with Maurice were the best years of my life. They were worth more to me than thirty years with the wrong person. I knew love Alfie, and it was better than any bloody thing life had to offer,' explained Margot, with a tear in her eye and passion in her voice.

'I'm so sorry. I never knew Margot,' said Alfie, touching her hand with empathy.

'Don't feel bad for me Alfie, it's a long time ago. I'm eighty-one now and I will see him again on the other side, of that I'm sure,' said Margot, with her face bursting into a smile at the thought. 'I want that for you boy, do you get it?'

'I do, I understand fully,' nodded Alfie. 'You are like my second mother Margot and I just want to thank you for being there for us as kids.'

'I only wish I could have done more lad, but I was on in years, and my health wasn't great. You were the one that did it Alfie, with your father. You raised those boys, and you, only a child yourself at the time,' she said, sadly. 'Now look at me and hear me when I tell you, you are special, so very special, the town adores you. You're our golden boy and we treasure you. Find a girl who is special too and worthy of your love.'

'How will I know she is the one?'

'Oh boy you will know. It will be clear as day. She will occupy your mind to such a degree you will want to charge her rent,' laughed Margot.

'That sounds like torture,' laughed Alfie.

'Remember what I said Alfie. Now go pack your bags and go find your new life. You always had a voice full of passion and beauty. You will have them eating out of your hand.'

'Thanks for everything Margot. Apart from Mum, you are the greatest lady I have ever known. Now I'm going to cut your lawn before I go, and say nothing about it.'

'I won't lie, I'd bloody well love it, thanks Alfie,' said Margot, touched by his gesture.

He went out to her shed, took out the lawnmower and cut her lawn. He spent five hours in her garden tidying up the whole place, trying to make it pleasurable for her. It was now seven o' clock and he looked at the peeling paint on the front of her house, and promised himself he would tend to that on his next visit home. He was due to leave for Cork the following day, but planned that he would return for a weekend to Galway after a month in Cork.

Yep, that will do for today. He headed home tired, but thrilled that he had given something back to Margot. A drop in the ocean of what she had given him, but it was something at least he thought, full of pride at his day's work.

11

Welcome to Cork boi

With his suitcase packed full of his most treasured belongings, and his guitar strapped to his back, Alfie boarded the train to Cork. It wasn't so hard to leave this time, as he knew home was only hours away, unlike his departure for the cruise ship. He had looked online at a rental agency, and had planned to meet a couple of guys who were interested in sharing a room. He had never been to Cork before, and when he arrived at the bus station, he liked what he saw. The river running along by the bus station made him feel at home. It was January, but instead of the usual rain and cold, he felt some winter sunshine on his face. He checked the maps on his phone for directions to the house in Industry Street. It was an attractive red brick, generous sized, terraced house. When he knocked on the door, a blonde guy answered.

'You must be Alfie. Welcome to Cork boi. Come on in now and sit your ass on the couch while we grill ya. I'm Tom, by the way.'

His other flatmate Pete came downstairs to greet Alfie too.

'What's the craic fella? So you are the Galway guy, not the Galway girl then?' joked Pete.

'That's the crappiest joke I ever heard,' said Tom. 'You know what he is doing don't ya, taking the piss out of that Galway girl song?'

'Yeah, I gathered that alright, haha. That is pretty bad in fairness,' laughed Alfie, feeling more comfortable with all the silliness surrounding him. The three boys went on to chat about their backgrounds, the house, and the house rules.

'You'll want a part-time job while you are doing that music course I suppose?' inquired Tom.

'I will, but thankfully I have a bit of money that I was saving for a rainy day behind me. That will sort me for now.'

'Right you are, now I have a buddy working in a café in town if you are interested,' said Tom.

'Definitely, I'd love it.'

'Don't worry we will sort ya out buddy. Now if you play us both a song and I mean a decent song, you can have the room,' said Pete, playfully.

'Ye guys are hilarious. I could do one by Tom Waits. Would that do?' asked Alfie, unsure of their taste in music.

'On the ball,' laughed Pete.

Tom agreed and Alfie played them the song, happy with the vibes that he was getting from them. He felt he was off to a good start and after the tune, he headed upstairs to unpack his bags. Not only had he found a great place to live, and a music course he was excited about, but it seemed he had also found two good friends to top it off. Every time his flatmates went out for a pint they invited Alfie along. The two guys were single, as was Alfie, and before long he had the women flocking around him again, but this time they were Cork women. He started the music course and was met by Ross, who showed him around. He liked the fact that it was an old type, red brick building, and Ross told him it was once a Catholic Boys School.

'I wondered about the significance of all those statues,' joked Alfie.

'I don't even see them anymore,' laughed Ross.

He familiarised himself with all the rooms especially his classroom. It was across from the canteen. A large room with chairs and tables and a stage at the end. He then walked across the hall, noticing a staircase on his right-hand side that he felt must lead to other rooms. He would investigate that later, but first he had to see the canteen. It was a huge old-fashioned room, like a hall with large windows and another stage at the end. The room was decked out with tables and chairs, and there was an old, steel exit door on the far side.

'Do you smoke Alfie?' asked Ross

'Yeah I do. I must give up at some stage though.'

'I'm going to show you now where to go for a smoke.'

Ross brought him to the old steel exit door and pointed to the space beyond.

'That's grand isn't it? I'd say you could get twenty-odd people out here at any one time?'

'Ah you could. You are not allowed to smoke anywhere else in the college. This is your spot.'

'No worries at all.'

'Class starts in thirty minutes, so let's go.'

Alfie glanced at Ross. He was a short man with brown, curly hair and glasses and had a very friendly face. He assumed he was about forty. He was very pleased that this guy was his teacher, and he felt he could even be friends with him in the future. He was right, because before long Ross had taken him under his wing entirely, and was spending lots of time making sure Alfie got ahead. He would always take a special interest in the students who demonstrated a real interest in learning, and Ross could see Alfie had tons of ambition.

'You're handy with that guitar Alfie. T'is like this, when you know one instrument well, you know them all. You just apply the same logic,' explained Ross, one afternoon.

Six months later, Alfie was playing Cello, Saxophone and Guitar to a high standard, and was now a level 3 in music theory. His hard work was paying off, and he was going for vocal lessons once a month to improve his singing skills. By now he was on friendly terms with his fellow students and teachers alike, and felt he was living his best life.

He was also working part time in a café, called Jolly Mude down in the city centre. It was a cool, popular, chilled out café that attracted the alternative types like artists, poets, and musicians. However, all types of people frequented it, as it was famous for coffees, pastries and healthy smoothies. The interior had palm tree wallpaper, wooden seats, bamboo art pieces hanging up, and milk bottle-shaped fairy lights hung from the main counter. When school finished at two o' clock, he would then go on to do his stint at the café, and later that night, time was allotted for his music. He was very busy, yet he found the time to enjoy all the female attention he got from the customers. A cute petite brunette called Emma was a frequent visitor to the café, and had her eye on him from first sight. She had been showering attention on him from day one, and he fancied her too.

'So when are you going to ask me out for a drink then?' she asked, on one of his shifts.

'We could go out tomorrow night if you are free? I finish my shift at 8 pm if that suits?' said Alfie.

'I'll be there,' said Emma, enthusiastically.

She felt he was a bit of a dark horse and wanted to get to know him better. Alfie tried his best to open up, bearing in mind what Margot had told him back in Galway. He wanted to see where it would lead, and he carried on seeing her for four months. By then she was becoming a bit demanding.

'Do you feel anything for me?' asked Emma, frustrated that Alfie didn't seem to love her.

'I like you Emma. We are having fun, but that's as far as it goes for now.'

'You never let me in Alfie, it always feels like you are not plugged in y'know.'

'I'm doing my best Emma. You're right. Maybe this isn't working and my heart isn't in it properly,' said Alfie, looking down at his toes.

'I'm done with this and I'm done with you. Good luck to whoever meets you. I've seen the way you are with women. You're just a player. Have you ever even been in love?'

'No, I guess I haven't,' replied Alfie, sheepishly.

He had tried so hard to open his heart since leaving Galway, and had dated girls on and off since he arrived, but he was really beginning to wonder if he would find anyone who would blow his mind. He decided it was time for a break from women.

Put the head into the studies fully. Despite the breakup with Emma and frankly, he was relieved about that, he felt life was going his way, and he began planning to go home every couple of months to see his family and Margot. He hadn't fully decided what he wanted to do with the music career, but he had ideas of joining a band with some of his classmates. Time was flying and he was focused completely on learning. A year into the course some people were starting to comment on how he was gifted, and his confidence was riding high. Life in Cork was all fun and games, and he didn't think it could get any better, until he was thrown a curveball in the shape of Georgia.

On a cold, February morning, he had innocently gone out to the smoking area of the college, ready for the usual cigarette, but became unearthed at the sight of Georgia on her first day. She had invoked feelings in him that he had never experienced before, and he loved it, but hated it all at the same time. Meeting her had made him feel as if he had switched from the driver's seat to the passenger seat in life. It looked as if she was about to take him on a journey, an exhilarating journey.

12

'Bring it on home to me'

'Earth to Alfie. Where did you go?' queried Ben.

'Em, sorry, I was deep in thought for a minute,' replied Alfie, realising he had been temporarily absent thinking of his mother, and how she called him her valentine.

'So, you're thirty-two Bee!'

'Sure I'm only a young slip of a thing. So, what were you thinking about? You looked very far away.'

'Oh, just my mother.'

'Aw, does somebody miss his mother? Have we a mammy's boy on our hands?' she joked, trying to lighten the mood that she felt had dropped a little.

'Oh, well I was a mammy's boy I guess, but she died when I was ten,' explained Alfie, with a serious look.

'Oh, no, I feel like such a fool. I didn't know, and I'm sorry for what I said just there.'

'Ah, it's cool. Sure how were you to know? She died of a heart attack at home when I was there alone with her.'

'So, you were there with her?'

'Yeah, I was, I couldn't help her unfortunately. It was all very sudden, but anyway never mind, it was a long time ago. What's in store for ye guys today?' he asked, swiftly trying to change the subject worried that Georgia and Ben would think he was vying for sympathy.

'Never mind us. That's really sad. I'm so sorry to hear that. You poor guy. I'm going to give you a hug,' said Georgia, with a sad face.

She threw her cigarette on the ground even though she had just lit it, and reached out her arms and wrapped them around Alfie's neck, and pulled him close to her as she did. As she hugged him, her face slowly brushed past his cheek, and he could feel her hair touching his. Her long, blonde hair cascading around his shoulders and chest. She felt warm, and he could feel his chest resting against hers, and he worried that she might realise how fast his heart was beating as they embraced. He put his arms awkwardly around her back to return the embrace, and felt his shoes touching her boots.

My first hug from her. Is this what it feels like to be in her arms? He wanted the moment to last forever, and just reach out for her face, and kiss her passionately. *If only Ben wasn't here, and if only she were mine, we could kiss God damn it. She's killing me.* Seconds had passed, and Georgia began to withdraw from the hug, and as she did, she looked him in the eyes sweetly. She took a step back and returned to her original position as if nothing had happened.

'That sucks buddy. I'm sorry to hear that. Life is a real bitch sometimes,' said Ben.

'Thank ye both, but let's move on. I've got a macho reputation to uphold here,' said Alfie, laughing, realising his face was flushed and he was feeling flustered.

Ben got the hint, and went on to talk about the upcoming summer concert for his class while Georgia listened in smiling. Georgia was touched by all this new information from Alfie, and had really enjoyed hugging him. It had come so naturally to her, and she had felt his heart beating fast, and a slight shake in his body when she pressed against him. She had sensed his nerves and shyness and it attracted her all the more.

Hmm, so you're a year younger than me, you can get all shy but I feel like I know you better now. Am I falling for him? Think I might be.

A few days later, Alfie had to go upstairs and as he climbed the steps, he heard singing, and he stopped to listen. It was Georgia. He hadn't heard her sing on her own since she was with Ben and Sid in the practice room, where he stumbled across them accidentally and fell in love with her voice. He could now hear her playing the piano singing 'Secret Garden' by Bruce Springsteen. He listened to her as she fumbled softly on the keys, knowing that she was still learning, and he heard her singing from the heart with all this feeling rebounding from her soul. She sounded like an angel to him.

That song could have been written for her. It's totally her. Holding onto a secret spot for herself alone where nobody else could touch. Whenever he looked in her eyes he always felt there was a slight distance between them, as if a pane of glass was separating them. *Intriguing, a mystery, but it's what makes you, YOU.* He didn't want to get caught listening to her, so he walked the last few steps and headed for the piano room. The music stopped abruptly.

'Hi, Alfie, don't tell me you were listening?' asked Georgia, looking unsure and slightly startled that somebody had heard her when she had thought nobody was around.

'I won't lie Bee, I heard it all. I think that song was written for you,' said Alfie, with a bashful smile.

'Really, why is that?'

'Ah it just suits your mysterious ways,' replied Alfie, with an even wider smile.

'Gee, I didn't know I had any. Sure I'm an open book.'

'Yeah, you are but there are a few pages torn out. Even so, it's a very interesting book, lots to discover.'

'One should never show all their cards Alfie,' laughed Georgia, with sparkling eyes.

'Oh, I think some people are worth the risk,' said Alfie, with his eyes beaming and his head slightly bent with a flirty smile. 'I must hand this into Bradley, but you sounded like an angel and I just had to stand and listen,' said Alfie, staring into Georgia's eyes.

'It's nice to hear that, thank you,' she answered. 'See you later, somewhere.'

'I hope so,' he replied, turning on his heels to continue to the piano room.

Later that day, classes finished for Alfie at 1.30 pm as Ross had an appointment. Alfie knew that Georgia's classes finished at this time, but his class always ran on until 2 pm, so he never seemed to get the opportunity to catch her on her way home. He decided he would wait outside until she came through the main door, and then he would casually suggest walking down the hill together. He got his bike and waited, chatting to some of the guys while expecting her to appear at any moment. His plan backfired when Seamus, one of the lads, pulled him into conversation about his money woes, and Alfie felt that he couldn't get away, so he was forced to watch Georgia come out the door, and breeze past him without even a look in his direction.

Damn it, I'm going to miss her now and I won't get to walk home with her.

Shortly after, Seamus got a call from a friend, and he told Alfie he had to run. Alfie took his bike and cycled down the hill, hoping to catch up with Georgia. He looked across the street and saw her admiring the Cherry Blossoms trees. Most of their flowers had fallen, but there was still some left on the trees. He got off his bike, and just stood there in a trance watching her, captivated by her beauty, and figuring that she must love these trees and their scent. He decided to head across the road in her direction, so he cycled right up next to her.

'They do say 'don't forget to smell the flowers as you go,' called out Alfie, getting off his bike and preparing to walk with her.

'Ah, yes, they… they the experts, that know everything. It's my favourite smell in the world and I wish I could stay smelling it all day, but then I would just look weird wouldn't I?' laughed Georgia.

'Weird isn't a word I'd use to describe you Bee. You should stay as long as you like' said Alfie, grinning.

'I just adore how all the pink petals line the ground as I walk through them. Pure Bliss. I'm easily pleased. Come closer and smell, and you will understand my obsession,' she said, as she leaned towards him touching his arm gently.

He tilted towards the pink Cherry Blossom tree and took a smell.

'Woah, I see what you mean. I wish I could hitch my tent right here now and bathe in the scent. It's divine,' he said, with a heavenly look on his face. 'I have to take a picture of you next to this tree Bee,' he said, reaching out for his phone.

'No, let's make it a selfie of both of us for the craic.'

He took the picture, and then reached for his keyring, and pulled out a penknife. He cut a tiny twig that had blossoms on it, and handed it to her.

'That's for you, now you can bring it home, and soak up the scent all you want.'

'Wow, thank you. I never felt like I could cut any of it off. It felt wrong, but now that you've done it, it's ok,' laughed Georgia, thrilled to bits with the courteous gesture, and a naughty smile crossed her face. 'You are quite the charmer Mister aren't you?'

'Ah sure I try! Are you going down along Bee?'

'Yeah, I have to meet a friend in town.'

They proceeded to walk together towards the city centre.

'So, I take it pink is your favourite colour then,' asked Alfie, keen to know more of Georgia's tastes.

'No, actually, I love every colour. They all have something to offer.'

'Even brown?'

'Brown is the colour of some leaves as they die, and then they line the streets, and you feel the rustling beneath your feet as you walk through them.'

'Do you see the beauty in everything?'

'Not everything, but most things. I remember being on holidays with my brother Oscar, and we were on the beach talking about good and bad, dark and light y'know?'

'Right, go on.'

'Well, as we sat on the boardwalk admiring the water, and having the best day, a yellow rose floated towards us. Oscar turned to me, and said 'look Georgia, that is obviously a yellow rose thrown in memory of somebody who died in the water. Isn't it beautiful? There's beauty in the darkness too, you just have to look closer to find it.' I never forgot it. It just resonated with me.'

'What a lovely story. I love how you express yourself, you are like a bloody poet,' replied Alfie, looking impressed and interested.

'A poet, you are joking! I just say what I feel,' replied Georgia, humbly.

'You are very insightful though.'

'I'm not really, I'm just a girl…. a girl standing in front of a boy asking him to love me,' she replied, breaking into a fit of giggles.

'I'm sorry, whenever I say I'm just a girl, it reminds me of Notting Hill, and I just love to take the mickey out of that quote,' laughed Georgia.

'You are funny Bee,' laughed Alfie, noticing how Georgia was trying to lighten the tone of their conversation.

'So when is that summer concert on? How's the practising going?' asked Alfie, swiftly changing the subject.

'It's all good, it will be on in June. You should come. We will be going for drinks after, and I say we should paint the town red that night,' said Georgia, excitedly.

'Try and stop me.'

By now they had reached the city centre.

'I gotta dash Alfie, people to see and all that. Have a great day. Nice talking with you.'

'Yeah, it's been fun. See you tomorrow.'

'If we are both still alive, I'll see you there.'

'Ah, I'd say we are safe enough.'

As Alfie cycled home, he felt like his brain had been blown. She was like no other woman he had ever known, and he felt like she healed the earth with her feet as she walked on it. She was like a bright light that had the power to turn a black rose into red just by touching it,' he thought to himself. When he was around her, he felt lighter and happier, and he figured that her radiance must be obvious to everybody who met her.

Yeah, I'm not the only one who sees it. There's lots of guys out there who are not blind to her charms, feeling threatened at the mere thought that someone could come along at any moment, and sweep her away. Right now he felt he had her attention, and he wanted to keep it that way. When he went home he decided to flop on his bed for a while, and just linger, looking at the picture he had taken of them both next to the Cherry Blossom tree. His mind began to drift and dream and he began to visualise all the things he wanted from her. As he looked at the two of them side by side in the picture, he thought about what it would be like for them as a couple. He would be happy with even the simpler pleasures of going to the cinema, out to dinner and even staying in to watch a movie and share a pizza together. He smiled as he imagined it. He pictured what it would be like to wake up next to her in the morning with her sleepy eyes and her hair all over the pillow. He wanted to feel her body against his and allow sleep to come knowing she would still be in his arms when morning light touched the bedsheets. He would give anything for it, but he wanted to love her more than he wanted to bed her.

Now that he had a photo of her, he finally had the chance to look at the other parts of her body, and notice the shape of her breasts which he could just about make out under the outline of her silk top. The curve of her tanned and toned legs, her shoulder bones, hips. He could stare as long as he wanted now. After a while of fantasising he fell into a deep sleep, as he had no work that day, and was free to indulge in his thoughts as he took an afternoon nap. Meanwhile, Georgia was in town waiting for her friend, and thinking about what had just happened with Alfie. She had loved their moment at the Cherry Blossom tree, but wished she could change everything after that.

You messed up there. He will think I'm hippy trippy and a bloody space cadet. I went too deep. No man can handle that, she shuddered to herself. *I hope I didn't turn him off now. I'm going to have to play it seriously cool for the next few weeks and regain the ground I just lost. I'll avoid him for a while, and hope that will work. You're slipping girl, slipping,* feeling frustrated she had played it all wrong.

The following day, Georgia made it her business to avoid Alfie in the smoking area, picking a different spot and chatting to some of the other students. When Alfie came outside she turned her head, and just tossed him a friendly wave, then continued chatting to the others. One of the guys in the group was a French student, about thirty-five, and in the class next door to her. She didn't know him as well as the other students, but they had exchanged pleasantries a few times, as he was relatively new to the place. He was very attractive, and he had proved to be a great hit with the girls. Georgia, however, had been too wrapped up in Alfie to care.

'Hi, Georgia, getting your fix?' asked Alexandre, the French student, in his perfectly smooth French accent.

'Ah, sure I am of course. Old habits die hard, and smoking is so glamorous isn't it?' she replied, sarcastically.

'It is when you smoke.'

'I doubt that very much. It's a rotten habit, and I need to give it up someday, but thanks all the same,' laughed Georgia.

'I thought you didn't smoke Alexandre,' said Johnny, a fellow student who was standing next to Georgia.

'I just needed a break and some fresh air I guess.'

'You won't find too much clear air out here buddy,' said Johnny, sarcastically, knowing full well Alexandre had just come out to talk to Georgia.

'So how is the ukulele practice coming along Georgia?'

'Oh, I'm spectacularly bad at playing. For what should be such a simple instrument, I just can't seem to get the hang of it. It's so frustrating.'

'I must get some notes for you from a friend of mine who plays it,' said Alexandre, looking helpful.

'That would be great Alexandre, thanks. Obviously, I want to be brilliant at it because I passionately love the instrument, but it's just not happening for me.'

'You passionately love everything,' scoffed Ger, another one of the lads. He was sixty-five and generally ignorant, and Georgia didn't care very much about him.

'I don't passionately love you Ger, now do I?'

'You do in my dreams' replied Ger, with a naughty laugh.

'And my nightmares.'

'Tell me Georgia, does the upstairs match the downstairs?' hollered Ger, fully realising that he was disrespecting her, and playing up to the audience of roughly ten guys around him.

'Pipe down my man. There's a lady present. Have some manners,' said Alfie, in an authoritarian tone.

'Thanks Alfie. You're sweet but don't worry, I've met plenty of creeps like this one. I can handle him. Ger, at least I have hair. Now, isn't it your bedtime? Time to tuck you up with some milk and cookies I'd say,' said Georgia, with a brazen smile, annoyed inside that she had been disrespected.

'I was only messing around George,' replied Ger, feeling a bit silly, and quickly noticing he had been met with disapproval from Georgia and the guys.

Georgia did not answer, and pretended as if nothing had happened, and resumed her small talk with Alexandre and Johnny. She didn't take joy in being mean especially about somebody's age, because truly she didn't care about such things, but she would not be anybody's fool. Tea break ended soon after, and she got back to her class with Alexandre walking alongside her, promising to bring the ukulele notes with him the next day. Alfie remained in the smoking area for some time after the others had returned to class. He couldn't quite decipher the swirl of emotions that were simmering in him.

Who's yer man. What's his game?' he wondered, perplexed at how the tea break had unfolded. *We just had that lovely chat yesterday, and she hardly looked at me today. God, she's hard work.* He was feeling jealous that she had spent her time standing away from him, and acting like he didn't exist.

13

'Because you're gorgeous, I'd do anything for you'

As the weeks flitted away, Alfie felt like he was getting the cold shoulder from Georgia. All she had been giving him was a friendly greeting, and a few words, and Alexandre seemed to be in the picture a lot more vying for her attention at every opportunity. Alexandre wasn't liked very much by the guys in the smoking area. Alfie would listen to them describe him as a bit snaky at times when he was out of earshot. The guys knew he was trying to get places with Georgia, and they didn't trust him. Alfie was trying not to give it much thought, and was doing his usual routine of going to the college, and then onto work until one day Georgia showed up with her niece at Jolly Mude's. He was making smoothies when he heard the bell ring. He looked up to see who had come into the café, and to his surprise, he saw Georgia standing there. She was wearing tight, black leggings with a stripy, low-cut top that hugged her figure underneath a long, brown, classy, woolly coat.

She looks like a million dollars, sexy as hell. But what is she doing here? He thought, feeling his face blush, and his blood pressure go through the roof. Georgia was with a

119

young girl who she later introduced as her niece. She sauntered up to the counter where Alfie looked gobsmacked.

'What the hell! I never knew you worked here,' said Georgia, looking uber-confident as always, but a little surprised.

'Yeah, I've been working here for the last year and a half. I've never seen you in here before, my God?'

'Such a cool café, I love it. I've been meaning to visit here for a while. Today, I was taking my niece out and she begged me to come in here. Ella, meet my friend from college, Alfie.'

'It's such a pleasure to meet you Ella, what a pretty name. How old are you?'

'Nice to meet you too Alfie. I'm 7.'

'Aren't you as lovely as your auntie! Now give me all your news, is she a nice auntie? I bet you're her favourite.'

'She's the best and she doesn't have any favourites. She loves us all the same.'

'Is that right now? I, for one am really glad you persuaded your aunt to come to this café today. What can I get you young lady? Whatever you want it's on the house.'

'What does on the house mean?' asked Ella.

'Haha, it means I'm buying,' said Alfie, pulling out all the stops to impress Georgia and her niece.

'No, Alfie, I can't have you do that.'

'Sit your butt down Bee, it's not up for debate. It's my treat.'

'That's so kind. Now, Ella, this is what a modern-day prince looks like.'

She took a seat with her niece and fell into conversation about toys and all little girl topics making sure to give her niece her full attention. As they drank their hot chocolate and ate their cookies, Alfie was busy serving customers, but stealing a glance at Georgia at every opportunity.

'I caught you looking,' said his co-worker Steve, gawping at Alfie.

'Did you? Oh no. There, my man, is the woman of my dreams.'

'I can see why. What a showstopper. Are you in with a chance though?'

'Jesus, I hope so.'

Just then Georgia happened to cast her eyes towards Alfie, and saw him staring at her.

You're gorgeous, but are you a heart breaker and a ladies' man? she wondered, totally impressed that he had been so kind to her and her niece. Thirty minutes passed, and Ella wanted to do some shopping, so Georgia took her by the hand, and headed to the counter once again to say goodbye to Alfie.

'Thanks again, you charmer. That was very sweet. My niece loves you.'

'I'll give her twenty cookies if she keeps that up.'

'Bye Alfie, thank you,' said Ella, beaming at the fun experience she had.

'Wait, Ella. Come behind the counter and pick something to take with you.'

'Really, wow, can I Georgie?' asked Ella, calling her by her nickname.

'If he says you can, go for it I guess,' replied Georgia, amazed at the special treatment Alfie was giving her niece.

'Pick anything at all,' said Alfie. with his arms stretched out.

'That pastry looks nice. Can I have that please?' asked Ella, completely excited to be behind the counter.

'Sold to the highest bidder.'

The little girl took her pastry and thanked him. Georgia was standing at the other side of the counter with the most luminous smile he had seen on her and her eyes were fixed on him.

'Come on Ella, let's go kitten. See you tomorrow Alfie. Love the café, and the service is top-notch.'

'Well, you will just have to come back, won't ye?'

With that, Georgia looked over her shoulder with a big grin, and off they went out the door.

'Err, she is so damn sexy. A woman has never had this effect on me. I don't even want to work now. I just want to swoon all day,' said Alfie to Steve.

'I know buddy, believe me. I hope you get lucky. Now get back to work Romeo.'

'Yeah, I will,' *but not before thinking about what a perfect mother she would make,* he dreamed. When he looked back towards the door, and the large window that was all condensation, he saw a love heart somebody had drawn with their fingers. It hadn't been there earlier. *Did Georgia do that? Damn, I wish I had been looking and not distracted by Steve.* As he worked throughout the day, he gazed at the love heart on the window until eventually the condensation cleared, and it disappeared.

The following day, Alfie repeated the same routine eager to see Georgia again, only to find she was once again on the missing list. He overheard Lewis her teacher tell the guys she had rang in sick, and might be missing for a few days. Three days came and went, and finally on Thursday she was back again in the smoking area.

'You're back Bee, I heard you were sick. Are you ok now?'

'Yeah, thanks. I'm back in the game. I never knew they were doing roadworks in my area, and ended up drinking dirty water. I was never so ill. I wanted to literally run away from myself, but obviously couldn't.'

'Oh, you poor thing, and who looked after you?'

'Well, I was chatting online to Alexandre, and he stopped by with soup and clean water. It was good of him. He didn't stay long.'

At that moment, Alfie felt jealousy like he had never known, and was utterly disgusted that not only had Georgia and Alexandre been chatting online, but he had called to her house aswell. He was pissed off, but couldn't let Georgia know.

This is what I get for not having a social media account.

'That was good of him,' said Alfie, through gritted teeth.

'Yeah, it was. Anyway, great news. Our lunchtime summer concert is tomorrow, and we will be going to O' Connell's bar afterwards. You can't miss it.'

'Oh right, yeah of course I'll be there. I'm looking forward to it. I've got to run Bee, I've got a lesson,' said Alfie, desperate to get away to indulge in his dark mood.

'Cool, see you tomorrow mister,' said Georgia, in a sunny tone.

This is war, outright war. That snaky fecker, getting in there before me with his online account, and calling to her damn house. Are they seeing each other now? What planet was I living on thinking I should take it slow. No, you don't Alexandre. I love her. What did I just say to myself? Love her. I do love her, and you are not going to get in my way Alexandre. It's time to let her know. I'm going to pull out all the stops tomorrow, and bring my guitar, and sing to her. It's happening,' he schemed, with determination taking him over entirely.

Friday beckoned, and Ross brought all his students, including Alfie, to the canteen for the lunchtime concert that Georgia's class was hosting. Alfie made his way to the front seats so that he had a perfect view of her, and as he glanced to his right, saw Alexandre in the same row. Georgia's class sang in groups and individually, and finally it was her turn to take to the stage. He watched in awe as she belted out a song he loved by Janice Joplin 'Take Another Little Piece Of My Heart.' Every note was perfect, and performed with zeal and feistiness. She looked at Alfie a few times, but was busy working the crowd and concentrating. He glanced over at Alexandre who looked as if he was drooling over her every move. The concert eventually drew to a close, and when the students got off the stage, he made a beeline for Georgia.

'That was passionate Bee, note-perfect.'

'Oh, thanks Alfie, passion is one thing I have in abundance. Too much even.'

'That's a great thing, you can never have too much passion. I love a passionate woman.'

'Ooo, tell me more.'

Without warning, Alexandre approached and interrupted their chat.

'If you sang like that in my country, you would be mobbed Georgia. All that energy was intoxicating,' said Alexandre, in his best flirty French accent.

'Ok, now I'm getting self-conscious. I'm going to head on over to your classroom Alfie.

They have classes on electronics going on there today,' said Georgia, looking embarrassed.

'I've signed up for another class upstairs. Damn,' spat Alexandre.

'Ah, I'm sure you will learn a lot up there Alexandre,' said Alfie, thrilled.

'Bee, I signed up for the electronics workshop aswell. See you there in a minute.'

She smiled and headed to the class, and took a seat next to her buddy and classmate Ben, and began to concentrate on the lesson. She was highly ambitious, and always focused on her lessons trying to put the wheels in motion for the day she would be a piano teacher. The class was scheduled to last for an hour. Twenty minutes in, her concentration began to lapse slightly, and she took a look around the room to see Alfie on the other side staring in her direction.

Is he staring at me right now or am I imagining it? Maybe he just thinks I'm sound. She turned away and then looked back again moments later to find he was still staring at her smiling, oblivious to what the teacher was saying. *Yep, its almost bold, he's flirting and letting me know he likes me, definitely. He hasn't taken his eyes off me this entire time. It's sexy as hell but I can't keep his gaze. I'm not used to him being so forward. I love it, but aah I feel nervous now,* thought Georgia, looking awkward and playing with her fingers.

In Alfie's mind, *it was time to step up the programme, and there would be a lot more to come today.* When the Electronics class ended, everybody headed upstairs to another workshop. This one was about acting. Georgia headed up the stairs with Ben pretending nothing had happened not even looking in Alfie's direction, and took her usual seat in her classroom. A few minutes later, Alfie breezed in smiling and headed in her direction.

Jesus, is he going to sit behind me now with all the available seats around? I'm dying with nerves. Come on Georgia. Stop losing your shit. Alfie took the seat behind her, and touched her on the back.

'Hey, you, are you stalking me?' asked Alfie

'Actually, yeah I am, I know where you live too, and I'll be waiting in the shadows later,' chuckled Georgia, bursting into a fit of giggles.

'Hahaha, so that was you the other night standing by the streetlight holding a sharp knife?' said Alfie, belly laughing.

'Damn, I never knew you saw me. I've got to be more ninja-like,'

The acting teacher walked in, and asked the class to quieten down.

'Yeah, quieten down Alfie, you're being very naughty,' said Georgia, in a sarcastic tone.

'You ain't seen nothing yet girl.'

Georgia turned her head to face the teacher, and got down to being serious and focused on the lesson. After about thirty minutes, she felt Alfie touch her hair like a gentle breeze. She got nervous and turned around to face him.

'Did you just touch my hair?'

'Haha, no, I'd say your classroom is haunted. Must have been a ghost,' whispered Alfie, with a naughty smile.

Georgia smirked and turned back again.

Hmm, nice, he is giving me a run for my money today isn't he? When class ended, everybody was in a rush to head for O' Connell's pub down the hill, about five minutes away.

'You coming Alfie?' called out Ben.

'Yeah, definitely, I must grab my guitar, and I'll meet ye all down there.'

'Cool,' added Georgia, just about concealing the excitement bubbling up inside her.

Tonight is the night.

14

Standing at the crossroads

A group of about fifteen students made their way to the pub. It was a small, cosy Irish traditional bar, and the students brought their different instruments with them. Georgia grabbed a stool next to Ben, and the pints began flowing bringing the craic with it. Each student took it in turn to sing a song, and after about an hour, Alexandre came into the pub. He stole Ben's seat next to Georgia while Ben was at the bar. He was an excellent conversationalist, and a complete intellect, and Georgia was very taken with these attributes, and felt at ease in his company. Her defences slipped somewhat as she continued to drink, and she and Alexandre got deeper and deeper into conversation. He confided in her that he felt increasingly lonely for his family in France, and how he hoped to find a girlfriend in Ireland, someone to settle down with.

'You are so interesting Georgia. I know so many are aware of your beauty, and I can certainly see why, but I like you for your intelligence.'

'That is so nice to hear Alexandre. I would prefer to be liked for that reason. Looks fade, and they are fleeting, but I'm the kind of girl who has to fall in love on an intellectual level first.'

For the next couple of hours, Georgia forgot about everyone else, and as the drink flowed they got lost deep in conversation.

He seems so solid and kind, and somebody who could protect me, and much as I'm perfectly capable, it would be nice to be looked after for a while. She glanced around the room to see Alfie sitting across from her talking to some of the guys. He suddenly picked up his guitar, and started to sing 'When A Man Loves A Woman' by Percy Sledge. It was the first time she had heard him sing, and was completely bowled over by the warmth in his voice. She gave him her full attention, and mid song noticed how he looked at her intensely.

Is he singing that to me? God I can't tell.

Georgia was a humble character who had a habit of mixing up the signals she got from men. She found it difficult to establish whether they had a crush on her, or whether they just thought she was a nice person. It was hit and miss a lot of the time, and her friends often said she needed to be hit on the head with a hammer to help her work out which was which. She recognised that she was very attractive, but she was also aware that she was just one of many, and as they say, beauty is in the eye of the beholder. She wondered whether her time as an ugly duckling had skewed her willingness to accept a man's interest in her, and resigned herself to the fact that she would always have a problem establishing what men's intentions were. As she looked closer at Alfie, she decided it was time to make a decision either way. Her gut instincts were screaming at her to choose, or at least find out which one she wanted it to be.

If they both like me, and I think they do, then it wouldn't be fair to keep them on a string, and the truth is I'm a little lonely for love. She had been single for six months now, and hadn't even gone out on a date yet. She could feel her heart flutter as she watched Alfie. He was just her type, so handsome, fun and caring, but her mother's words trickled through her mind. *'Never go for the player type George. They'll break your heart. They will be out in the pub flirting with the ladies, and they will tear you in half. Pick the reliable guy. Yeah, he might be less exciting, but he will treasure you, and care for you, and love is caring. Remember that.'* Her mother had learnt this lesson on her own dating journey before she met Georgia's father Harry. *I can't risk it, I want to, but I can't. I can't have you break me. How can I trust you? If you take me down will I even be able to get back up again? Yeah, you say all the right things, but you probably do that to every woman. I'll be a novelty for a while, and then you will throw me away like a used toy, or just sleep with me and leave me. I can't have that.*

As always, at that moment, relying on her instincts she made a snap decision. When it came to making choices Georgia always trusted her gut instincts, but down the road she was to find out they weren't always right, and that she had made the worst possible decision.

I'll choose Alexandre. He won't let me down. He likes me for my brains as well as my looks, and he will make great boyfriend material. Alfie finished his song, and smiled affectionately at Georgia.

'What an impressive singer. My oh my, is there anything you are not brilliant at you fecker?'

'Ah, there is, I'm not brilliant at getting the lady I want.'

130

'I'm sure you will find your princess one day,' she laughed, getting up off her chair and heading for the bar before Alfie could respond.

Alexandre followed her and put his arm around her.

'I'm a little drunk, but I must ask you something. Can I kiss you right now?' begged Alexandre, with a longing look.

'I'd like that,' replied Georgia, and with that he leaned in, and they kissed passionately at the bar in full view of all the students, customers and a shocked Alfie.

Oh my good God, did that just happen? Did she just kiss that snake? You have to be kidding me. Screw you Georgia, screw everything. I'm done, decided Alfie, vicious that the night he had planned to make his move had completely blown up in his face. He felt the jealousy rip through his body, and looked back at Georgia again in disbelief wondering if his eyes had deceived him. Georgia and Alexandre had now taken a breath, and Georgia turned back and headed towards her table as all the students cheered and clapped. She noticed the look on Alfie's face was one of confusion and jealousy, but she wondered if she was just imagining it. Suddenly, Alfie got up and grabbed his guitar.

'I must head off guys. I just got a text from my flatmate saying he forgot his keys, and can't get into the house. See ye tomorrow,' he lied, and off he stormed out the door without a second look at Georgia.

Alfie grabbed his bike, and walked into town beside it realising he was too drunk and upset to cycle. He felt numb as if his brain had exploded into a million, tiny, sharp little pieces.

How did it all go so wrong? When he eventually got home, he flopped into bed and just slept. He was worn out from all the anger, confusion, and despair that had raged within him. The next day, all he could do was lie on the couch, and watch TV. He called in sick, and tried to concentrate on a movie, but he was consumed by thoughts of Georgia and Alexandre.

His flatmate Tom wandered into the sitting room, and was amazed to see Alfie lying there.

'I thought you had work today Alfie?'

'Yeah, I called in sick. I couldn't be arsed. I mightn't bother going in tomorrow either.'

'That's not like you, did something happen?' asked Tom, concerned.

'You know that girl Georgia? She kissed one of the guys from the Abbey last night there in the bar, and right in front of me. Can you bloody well believe it?' ranted Alfie, with his face like thunder.

'Oh, no, you are kidding me. I thought you were getting places with her. Who the hell is yer man?'

'I thought I was getting places too, he is a French student who goes to the Abbey. Apparently they have been chatting online for weeks, and hanging out. I loved her. It's the first time I've been in love with a woman, and now this,' stressed Alfie, exasperated at the thought.

'Oh, man, I know you did. Believe me buddy, I know how it feels. I've had women take a short cut through me aswell, it's agony.'

'That's fair enough Tom, but this changes everything.'

'Like what? You just need to forget her mate. Forget her.'

'I don't know man, my brain is going to some dark places right now. I'm thinking of heading back to Galway.'

'Whaat? Are you mad? Over a woman?' You are talented at that music Alfie, don't go giving it up for her. This will pass buddy. Give it a few days, believe me. Don't go making rash decisions now for God's sake,' begged Tom, horrified at the idea of losing his friend.

'Thanks Tom and I know you have my back. You and Pete have been phenomenal to me. I know it, believe me, but something is telling me to get up, and get the hell out of here now.'

'Just give it a few days please. Cork wouldn't be the same without you here,' pleaded Tom.

'Ok, look, I'll think it over for the next few days, but no more than that alright?'

'Good man yourself. A lot can change in a few days. I'll get you a beer from the fridge, and we'll watch something on the box. I've got your back.'

'Make that twenty beers,' joked Alfie, with a hint of a smile.

'See there it is, a smile. You'll be laughing again soon.'

'I doubt that very much,' replied Alfie, utterly depressed.

Alfie's mood failed to lift over the weekend, and instead he found himself getting more angry at the situation. When Monday arrived, he headed up to the college, but this time he would not go to the smoking area to see Georgia. No, now he would avoid her at all costs. He spent the next few days being much quieter in class, lost in thought as to what road in life he should take now. Would he stay or leave? He couldn't decide, but he hoped the answer would become clear soon.

On his free evenings, he would scour the internet searching for ideas, and looking at what courses were available in Galway. It was only June, and they would start in September, so there was still time to figure this one out, he reckoned. At this stage, a week had passed, and while taking a walk around the city centre, the answer hit him.

Marine Science. He had seen the course advertised in Galway University, and it was starting in September. He reflected on his time on the cruise ship, and how all of the other aspects of the ship had interested him, and now he had an opportunity to explore them further. *I've got the brains, I can do this. I'll forge out a career for myself, make good money, and never get distracted by a woman again. Pops was right all along. Stick with your career.* He saw a coffee shop, and decided to get on his phone, and apply for the course right there. *That's it now, no turning back. All they have to do is say yes, and all I have to do is quit the music course. I'll show her.*

Hurt, anger and rejection had become the motivator and ruler of his plans, and he was thinking rashly. Another week passed, and Monday morning came around. He had a spring in his step, and he was excited at the idea of quitting the course, and rubbing Georgia's nose in it at break time. He had it all planned out step by step. First, he told Ross in the morning that he was super grateful for the opportunity he had been given, but he felt he had got all he needed from the experience, and was now keen to change direction, and study in Marine Science in Galway.

'I thought you were loving it here. I'm really surprised, but you know I support you in all you do. You are a gifted student Alfie,' said Ross, surprised and disappointed as he was about to lose one of his favourite students. 'Have you been offered a place on the course?'

'Yeah, I have thankfully. My Uncle works in the college, and pulled some strings. You were my favourite teacher Ross, and you are also a good friend. I'm going to miss you, but today is my last day,' declared Alfie, feeling guilty at springing his news on Ross with no notice.

'Ok, I'll get the paperwork ready, but Alfie, don't be a stranger. A lot of people think the world of you here, and they will be sad to hear this. They really will.'

'I majorly appreciate that Ross, and I'll be in Cork again for sure,' lied Alfie.

He had no intention of coming back again.

Be back my ass. Cork has kicked me good, or at least Georgia has, but hey, what's the difference? He arrived into the smoking area at tea break having missed the last week.

'Hey, Stranger, where have you been?' I haven't seen you around. I thought you had given up the smokes?' asked Georgia, enthusiastically.

'Yeah, I was trying to, but they got the better of me today.'

'What you been up to?' asked Georgia, with her usual charming smile.

'Ah, not a lot. I'm starting college back home in Galway in a few months,' said Alfie, casually.

'You are?' I'm dumbfounded! I thought you'd be here for at least another year,' she said, completely horrified at the new information.

'Sure, I've been here a year and a half, and it's been brilliant, but I've taken it as far as I want to.'

'But what about the music?' 'I thought you were going to form a band,' said Georgia, knocked for six thinking he would be around for ages yet.

'Yeah, I changed my mind I guess. This course will be a really good opportunity for my career, and I would be mad to pass it up y'know?'

'Oh. What is the course? I'm sorry, I'm just flabbergasted.'

'It's Marine Science. As you know I worked on a cruise liner and it just fits,' said Alfie, thrilled that she was looking horrified.

'Oh, ok, right, em.. 'When are you leaving? A couple of months from now?' stammered Georgia, looking worried at what she was going to hear next.

'Today, actually,' said Alfie, with a smile.

'Today! Whaat? So, this is your last day? I can't believe it. Are you leaving Cork today too?' gasped Georgia.

'Yeah, my flatmates know about it. I'm leaving tonight so yeah, upwards and onwards,' professed Alfie coolly, with no emotion.

'Oh. So this is goodbye then? Alfie you will be missed,' said Georgia, with a face that looked like she had been kicked in the stomach.

Georgia reached out to try and hug him, but as she did so, Alfie stood back unpredictably.

'I'm not great at goodbyes Georgia. Good luck on the course. I have to go now,' he called over his shoulder as he turned to leave.

'Georgia, who is she?' I thought I was Bee,' said Georgia, amazed.

'Uh, yeah,' replied Alfie, walking through the steel exit door without turning around.

Georgia stood there watching him leave bewildered at what had just taken place. *What in the name of Jesus? What have I done choosing Alexandre? I love Alfie for Christ's sake, and now I've blown it. You've really done it this time girl. But if he was into me like I think he was, he didn't fight for me, did he? You've made your bed, now lie in it. Why was he so cold just there? And he never called me Bee*, still having trouble digesting all that Alfie had said. There were so many questions, and she knew she would have to let the answers flow over her in their own time.

She continued to meet Alexandre for the next few weeks going on dates, but apart from a few kisses, it was going nowhere. As time went by, Alexandre grew quieter and then stopped messaging her online, and began to avoid her on the course. Then, one day shortly after, as he headed to the office, she stopped him in the corridor.

'Hey, you, I haven't heard from you lately, you've been very quiet.'

'True, I've had some things I'm dealing with. I'm just not in a good place right now for this Georgia.'

'Don't say another word, I knew it. I knew you had lost interest. It was a mistake for us to get together'.

Was I mad? She thought, fuming inside at how he had messed her around, and blew her chance with Alfie.

'It's not you Georgia. I just don't think I can be in a relationship right now,' said Alexandre. The truth was that he recently seen another woman he would like to date, and was eager to explore that possibility.

'I understand fully. It's fine. Hopefully we can be friends in the future,' said Georgia nonchalantly, deciding that she had to be classy for her own sake.

'You are so understanding. Thanks for being so kind Georgia. I do hope we can remain friends.'

'Cool, I gotta run now. Chat to you soon.'

She had other classes to attend as it was only 12 o'
clock, and school finished at 1.30 pm, so she went to the
bathroom to give herself a chance to think. She looked at
herself in the mirror, and took a deep breath. After com-
posing herself, she decided to go home early, but then remembered her school bag was upstairs in the classroom.

*If she went back up to get it, she would be questioned as
to why she was leaving, and that wasn't going to happen.* She
rummaged in her pocket and realised she had her wallet
and keys on her. *Screw the bag, I'm outta here,* she decided,
and took to the front door, and headed for home. *Screw
him, he is dust now. Absolute flipping eejit. I'm taking a few
days off to chill my brain, and I don't care about the con-
sequences,* she thought boldly. When she got home, she
reached for her phone only to realise she had left it in her
bag in the classroom. *Damn, no phone. Actually, I don't
bloody care about that either. Anyone who wants to ring my
phone, go on. I couldn't give a shite,* now fuming at how her
day was going, and how she had been discarded like trash
by Alexandre. *This dating lark is a load of crap.*

For the next few days, she lay low, but decided to go
back to the Abbey on Friday just to get her phone. When
she arrived, people were surprised to see her.

'Where were you Georgia? You had us all worried.
You were gone for three days and your bag was here. We
couldn't get you on the phone either,' said Ben, looking
concerned.

'Thanks for your concern Ben, but I was just taking a
bit of time out,' said Georgia, looking dejected and mis-
erable.

'What do you mean Georgia? What's going on with
you right now?'

'Ben, I don't like to be around people when I'm in a mood, and right now I'm in one, but I don't want to say why. Can we just leave it at that?'

'Ok, but can I do anything?'

'No, but thank you. I just have to let this storm rage for a while. I'll be grand again soon. I'm just fed up right now.'

'Ok, well, I'm here ok?'

'I know babes.'

For the next few weeks, Georgia took more time off explaining to her teacher that she wasn't feeling the best. A storm had been brewing in her since her breakup with Jesse, but all this time she had been distracted by her love of music and Alfie. It was time for her to pay her debts, and these debts didn't relate to money. They were the outstanding feelings she had buried deep within her while she had chosen to take the path of denial for the last six months. What goes down must come up, and at one fell swoop thoughts of fear, isolation, anxiety and loneliness began to emerge at full throttle.

15

Down, down, down she goes into the rabbit hole

Georgia carried on each day taking her usual route to the college, but now her legs were feeling heavy as she walked up the hill, and crazy thoughts out of nowhere were taking over her brain. One morning out of the blues, a notion popped into her head.

Throw yourself under that bus. It frightened her to the core. *Where did that come from? I'm not suicidal.* This was the beginning of her experiencing intrusive thoughts, something she had never heard of, but would come to understand much later. These thoughts would take the shape of everything dark and scary, attaching themselves onto the people she loved most. It was like a cruel joke was being played on her by her own mind. While at class, she began to experience hot and cold sweats, and couldn't concentrate on her lessons. It was getting harder and harder, to keep up the pretence that everything in life was dandy, because it wasn't. Life was fast becoming a living nightmare, and she didn't feel she could confide in anybody. In her mind, she had to be strong and weather the storm. Lewis had noticed she wasn't being herself, and asked her if they could have a chat at breaktime. They found a corner away from everyone in the smoking area, and she looked into his compassionate eyes, and decided to tell him the truth.

'I feel as if I'm cracking up Lewis. I'm shaking all the time. My heart rate is through the roof. It's like my nervous system has gone haywire. I feel like there's no foundation underneath me anymore. It's like the ground has come away, and I'm hanging by a thread in thin air,' explained Georgia, with tears in her eyes.

'It's anxiety Georgia, that's what's going on. You need to see a doctor. I promise you will get through this, but you need some help with it,' said Lewis, in a soothing, reassuring tone.

'Anxiety? But I don't get anxiety.'

'Everybody gets it at some stage Georgia. You've had a lot to deal with. You're not long out of a six-year relationship, and you are living on your own now. It's a lot to contend with.'

'Maybe. Thank you so much Lewis. I'm sorry if I burdened you. I will go see my doctor, and think about what you said.'

'Burden me? Are you kidding? I want to help. Keep me in the loop. You've become a really good friend to me, and I care about you,' said Lewis, with kindness radiating from him.

A few days later, she was sitting in her doctor's office, a young, thirty-something, good looking, highly educated doctor with a distinctly impressive bedside manner. She sat in front of him shaking like a leaf with panic written all over her face.

'I don't know what's wrong with me. I can't sleep and I can't sit still. My arms look completely strange. My breath is in my mouth and my legs feel heavy like tree logs. I feel like I'm cracking up. My friend thinks it's because I broke up with my boyfriend of six years over six months ago. I think he might be right. Please help me.'

'I'm observing your body language, and listening to you Georgia, and what you are experiencing is severe anxiety. Your arms are mottled because your circulation is being hampered. You've been through a trauma it seems, and you haven't dealt with it properly, and now it's all coming to the surface. I think counselling is the best course of action.

'Oh, there's no way. It's out of the question,' said Georgia.

'That's a shame. Right, I can give you some valium to help calm you down, but these pills are highly addictive, and should only be used short term.'

'Ok, if you think it will help, great,' said Georgia, relieved.

They continued with their discussion, and she discovered she had been experiencing, without her knowledge severe panic attacks, up to ten a day. Things were becoming a little clearer, and Georgia decided she would take one tablet every morning while she continued to go to the Abbey, but things weren't getting much better. The panic attacks were almost daily, aswell as up to thirty intrusive thoughts. On the surface, everyone around her thought she was as calm as ever, and some students even complimented her on her calm composure, saying how much they envied her for it. Georgia was relieved that at least externally nobody could see the real pain that she was going through. She had an act to uphold, and was desperately trying to appear as if she had it together.

Her usual smiling ways and sunny nature had however diminished somewhat, and some of her closer friends from class were curious as to where her famous megawatt smile had gone. During classes, she would take time out to go to the bathroom in order to get in a few deep breaths, but nothing was working. She continued to miss days, and was now visiting her doctor weekly for reassurance. His kind words would help her for a couple of days, and then gradually fade away leaving her back in the same old panicked situation. One afternoon, while speaking with the doctor, she asked him more about the panic attacks.

'I know they are like a loss of control and can be brutal. Have you ever experienced them before all of this?' he queried.

'Now that I think of it, yes. I was in Sydney, Australia a few years ago, and was with my ex at the time when I began to feel unsafe because of horrible stories a girl had shared with me. I began to feel very paranoid, and my boyfriend had to take me to my happy place, which was in Bondi Beach, and help bring me round. I was in such a state, and in order to calm me, he had to point out kind looking people on the beach. He would say 'Look Georgia, there's a man walking his dog on the beach. Does he look as if he would harm you? Other times he would point out senior couples holding hands and laughing together, anything to bring me around, and it helped a lot. I could see his logic. However, later on, when we went back to a hotel in Bondi and I climbed into bed, I got completely freaked out. I explained to Jesse at the time, that it was like a blanket of fear that crept from my toes right up to my neck and made me feel as if I was going to smother or drown. When it reached my neck I felt as if I would die,' explained Georgia, horrified to revisit such an awful event.

'Yes, Georgia, that is a panic attack, but you survived it, didn't you? And all of the ones you had lately. You didn't die did you?' asked the doctor.

'No, you're right, I didn't.'

'See, that's the thing, you think that they will kill you, but they don't. It's just an influx of stress hormones. Look, Georgia I'm completely here for you, and I genuinely feel for you. You have been coming to me for years, and you're always such a little force of nature, and now I see you broken, it makes me feel bad. I promise that you can continue to see me each week, and I'll try to make you feel better. I will do that, but ultimately I feel there are some deep issues that need sorting, and only counselling will do that. I know I mentioned it before but would you consider going if I give you a number?'

'I've always said I would never go for counselling, but you've given me a lot of your time, and I appreciate it so much, so maybe I need to break my rule, and go check this out. Anything to make this crap stop.'

This was a big move for her, but she felt she had leaned on her doctor for far too long, and she was determined to fix her own problem even if it meant the dreaded counselling. She feared that maybe they would try and implant ideas in her head or mess with her thinking in some way. She had heard the horror stories, but she knew she had to give it a try. She made an appointment at a counselling office called 'New Starts' in the city centre on the recommendation of her doctor. She had no idea what to expect, and went to the building which was a little run down and pressed the buzzer. She went up a narrow stairs, and sat in a tiny waiting room. While waiting she observed her surroundings; white walls and multiple posters on a notice board all relating to mental health. Georgia looked at the posters with a sense of disdain and cynicism that even she herself, could not quite articulate or understand. The term 'mental health' had become a catch-all phrase, both vague and stigmatising and she deflected her eyes away from the posters, towards her feet, feeling exposed as if she was sitting under a flashing, neon sign, advertising exactly why she was there. There was classical music playing in the background, and she didn't understand why, but it was irritating the hell out of her. She just played with her phone trying to distract herself from all the annoyances surrounding her. After a little while, a friendly-looking lady eventually arrived and greeted her with a smile.

'Hi Georgia?' she enquired.

'Yes, that's me,' replied Georgia, nervous at the whole situation.

'I'm Hanna, your counsellor and I'm delighted to meet you. Please come into my office and take a seat.'

'Thank you.'

She looked into the office, it was a generous sized room, like a big sitting room. It had two comfy looking green chairs a few feet apart facing each other in the middle of the floor. The walls were a soft white colour, and she observed a large window on the front-facing wall. The window was slightly open, and she could hear noises from outside. Buses passing by, people mumbling, cars beeping. All the sounds of the city, and to her they were a little comforting, almost the sound of normality, a sound she was used to.

'Which seat do I take?'

'Whichever one you wish.'

'Ok, I'll take the seat on the right side. I don't know what it is about the right side, but I always have to take it. I used to get annoyed with my ex whenever he walked on the right side. He kept on forgetting, and it used to drive me mad,' laughed Georgia.

'Oh, that's funny. What happened when you sat on the couch or lay in bed? Did it have to be on the right side?' asked Hanna, looking amused.

'Yep, always the right side,'

'That's a new one for me. I'm enjoying you already.'

As Hanna stood up to get her pen and paper ready, Georgia studied her appearance. She was tall and slim with long, brown hair, lovely brown eyes and a friendly smile. She looked to be in her late twenties, and gave the impression of being very mature and responsible.

'So, Georgia. I'd like to tell you a little about myself. I'm from Lithuania, and I've lived and worked in Cork for the last five years. I'm twenty-eight, and I trained in Lithuania as a psychologist. So, would you like to tell me a little about yourself?'

'Sure. I've lived in the city for many years, and I've never been for counselling before. This is my first time, and it's very strange. My doctor sent me here because he thinks I may have a panic disorder, and that I also suffer from severe anxiety. I broke up with my ex over six months ago, after six years together. I'm finding it extremely difficult to function at the moment, so yeah, that's me,' said Georgia, sitting upright in the chair suddenly looking rigid, nervous and defensive.

'Ok. Thank you so much for sharing that with me. Right, first things first, would you like to discuss the past with me or is it just the present we are dealing with?'

'I hadn't thought about that, but really I'm ok with the past. It wasn't a bed of roses, but I'm ok with it. I'd like to deal with the present because that's what is pulling me down at the moment,' said Georgia biting her lip.

'I see, that's no problem. The type of therapy I practice is called CBT; short for Cognitive Behaviour Therapy. It has been shown to be quite effective for anxiety, and it also helps by giving you coping strategies. I'll give you a leaflet that will go through it in more detail after our session today.'

'Ok, well obviously this is all new to me. I've got to wrap my brain around it. If I keep coming to you will you be able to help me? Will you be able to make these panic attacks stop?'

'I certainly hope so. I've helped many people over the years with this problem, and many of them are living happily now working jobs, and have recovered greatly. Now, let's talk about you. What's going on and what are you experiencing every day?'

'Actually, I feel as if I can't breathe a lot of the time. In fact, I'm having trouble breathing right now. I think I might be about to have another panic attack. I can't believe this. My heart is racing, and I'm freaking out.'

'Ok, ok. It's ok. Just breathe with me. It's all going to be ok. You are in a safe place now. Just take deep breaths with me right now. In through your nose and out through your mouth, nice and slowly,' said Hanna, calmly and in control.

Georgia was hyperventilating, but listened to Hanna instantly, and took deep breaths in and out with her for a few minutes, and the symptoms began to subside.

'Now, it's passing isn't it?'

'Yeah, I think it might be. I'm so embarrassed exposing myself in this way. I normally go to a private place to suffer alone.'

'And you don't confide in anybody, and let them help you?'

'No, I can't. I have to be strong at all times. I can't let them see me vulnerable. I just have to hold it together no matter what. I must always be in good form, and strong for others.'

'You might be surprised to hear this Georgia, but the people who are strongest mentally are those who open up and share their problems, not those who keep them hidden. They are more at risk.'

'Really? I'm surprised. I want to be one of the mentally strong people. I think I was, up to this point in my life. It seems so very far away right now, oceans away.'

'I know it does, but every time you come here, and you do your homework for me, I promise you, it will become closer.'

'Homework? I don't understand,' laughed Georgia.

'Haha, you weren't expecting that. Yes, you get homework. Don't worry, it's just little exercises to help you each week.'

'This is all so different. I don't mind telling you I hate homework, but if I must, I will. Maybe I should come twice a week so I can get better quicker?'

'I believe it's better if you only come for one session a week as it gives you time to process properly. One session a week is an excellent goal, and don't feel as if you have to be in such a rush to get better. These things take time, and you need to be kind to yourself.'

They proceeded to talk gently about all the strange things that were happening in Georgia's mind and body.

'My face goes numb sometimes, and I can't feel anything.'

'Yes, that can be a symptom of anxiety for sure. I would advise you not to fight it, but just sit with it. Tell me more,' probed Hanna.

'I study music about twenty minutes from here, and I go to a music college. Lately, I can't read my piano music properly. My vision goes without warning, and everything becomes blurry, and I see jagged lines. I go to look at my teacher Bradley, and most of his face disappears, and all I see is one of his eyes, and it terrifies me.'

'Of course, that would be hugely terrifying. How long does it last? And have you told your doctor?'

'It lasts for maybe a half-hour, and then I get a massive headache, and I just want to sleep it off. When it happens, I can literally hear my heart beat in my chest so loudly, and it feels like I'm being taken on a fast ride in a car, and I'm begging the driver to stop, but he won't. I hate it so much. I want to break down crying when it happens because it's such a loss of control, but I can only do that when I'm on my own. My doctor doesn't know what it is. He has done tests, but we haven't got to the bottom of it yet.'

'It's probably a symptom of stress, but obviously the doctor has to call that one. I must tell you that our bodies do crazy things in times of stress,' said Hanna, reassuringly. 'When did all of these things start Georgia?'

'It all started two months ago. I was seeing a guy and it didn't work out. I was in a bad mood over it for a few days, and then it just spiralled out of control over the weeks. One morning, as I was walking up the hill to the course, out of the blue, a thought entered my head to throw myself under a bus. It shook me to the core.'

'Oh, you have been through it you poor girl. Now, tell me when you had the thought, was there an intention to do it?'

'God, no, I was suicidal in my twenties, and I know what that feels like, but then I was knocked down by a car in Paris. I realised how precious life is, and it's the last thing I would ever do now. I completely saw the light!

'Ok, that's good, very good. Now have you had other thoughts like this?'

'Yes, loads of them, all day long. The doctor gave me valium, but I only take it in emergency's because I'm afraid of getting addicted, so I wait until I can't take it anymore and then I take a tablet.'

'Does that make them go away?'

'No, but it slows them down at least. It angers me so much that it doesn't make them go away as I get no break, but it's better than racing thoughts coming at a mile a minute though,' said Georgia, now tearing up.

'Do you think you could share more of the thoughts with me?'

'I think I can, but I'm deeply ashamed, and feel like a horrible person,' said Georgia, now bawling crying.

'You seem like an absolutely kind, charming girl to me. I don't believe you are horrible for one second. I have met all types of people, and I don't think that describes you, and I know we have only met today.'

'My thoughts are all very random, and my brain is not behaving as it did all my life. Ok, so I'm sensitive to bad words, evil words like kill, hurt, stab, anything that means bad. Now those words attach themselves to people's names.

It shakes my bones because it in no way stands for the real me, and how I think. I am kind. I believe in good, not bad. I would never hurt a fly, and it's like a cruel joke is being played on me. The worst kind of joke. I feel ashamed, guilty, and hate myself for thinking these things. This whole anxiety thing is hell on earth, but this is the worst part of it,' said Georgia, now sobbing uncontrollably.

Georgia was feeling shocked at the hollowness to her crying. She couldn't believe how deep her cries were reaching within her, and never remembered crying in such a way before.

'I understand, so there's never an intention to follow these thoughts, they are just racing thoughts?'

'Intention, God no. The exact opposite, and yes they are racing thoughts.'

'What you are experiencing are intrusive thoughts,' said Hanna calmly.

'What does that mean? I have never heard of such a thing,' asked Georgia, wide-eyed.

'They are completely harmless, and in no way a reflection of you. Your stress hormones are through the roof right now, and everybody experiences these in some way or another, but sometimes they spiral, and can really damage a person's life if they don't understand it. You don't want to do any of these things, but did you ever hear of the pink elephant?'

'No.'

'If I told you not to think of the pink elephant, you wouldn't be able to think of anything else but the pink elephant would you?'

'Hmm, yeah, it's true. I'm thinking of the pink elephant right now haha,' smiled Georgia.

'When you get these thoughts your body has a reaction to them, a bad reaction, and the brain senses that it must pay attention to them as if they are unresolved business. When you react, you blow something tiny into something huge, and then the brain just keeps revisiting it until you don't react anymore. Do you understand?'

'Yes, I'm listening,' said Georgia, now drying her tears.

'This is going to take work, but you must try to let them flow over you like clouds, and not react. It's going to take a lot of practice.'

'When they are coming, I stop them midways when I can.'

'Well, that's still a reaction.'

'I can't bear them entering my mind. I'm not going to lie to you, I can't let them flow over me. They disgust me, but what I can do is flip them.'

'So, right, how will you flip them?'

'I'll have to give it some thought, but if the word is murder, I could say burger straight after. It would make me feel better. If it's kill, I could say Bill. I'm feeling better already,' said Georgia, smiling.

'I'm delighted to hear that because as you understand them you will feel a lot better. The ultimate goal is to let them flow over you, but if all you can do right now is to flip them, and that makes you feel better, that's a start. I must tell you though that every human brain has thousands of thoughts every day, so you mightn't be able to catch them all on time.'

'Yeah, I realise that from trying to stop them halfway through. Some little buggers still got through,' laughed Georgia.

'Little buggers is right. They are like unwelcome visitors. Ok, our session is nearly up but I want you to start doing some reading on anxiety. I think reading other people's experiences will let you know you are not alone. I also want you to look at meditation apps as they can be really helpful.'

'How did today go for you Georgia? I'm aware that not every counsellor and client suit each other?'

'Well, I think it went brilliantly, and I'm so glad I got you. I can't tell you how much you have helped already. You are my person now. Is that ok with you?'

'I would be delighted with you as my client. Great, I'll see you next Friday, and we will see how you are getting on.'

'Thank you so very much Hanna' replied Georgia, gratefully.

As Georgia left the office she noticed the smell of lilies in the waiting area, and a smile spread slowly across her face.

16

'All the king's horses and all the king's men...'

As she walked home after the appointment, Georgia felt proud of herself for taking this leap of faith and remembered her mother's words.

Everything goes full circle. Now, if that is true, it means I will return to the old me at some point. I've just got to hold on, keep holding on, and pray that I won't be like this forever. Life is a series of phases, surely this is a phase. Christ, I hope so. She decided that she felt better when she kept moving, so every day after the music course finished at 1.30 pm, she would rush home, fuel up with food, and get out the door walking for hours on end, until her feet felt like they were burning, and she was too tired to walk anymore. She figured if she burned off the nervous energy, she might be able to relax a little more in the evening and have fewer panic attacks. The alternative was to stay at home listening to pan pipes or some form of relaxing music, but then her mind would spiral out of control, while she sat there tensed and horrified at the state of her life. She even played a song by John Denver from her childhood days to help her stay calm, but to no avail. When she was out walking, at least she got distracted by nature and by the people around her. She was at war with her own mind, and was trying endlessly to outsmart the intruder anxiety. One afternoon, while out walking, she decided to ring Jesse.

'Hey, Jesse, we haven't talked for a while. Just wondered if you would like to get a coffee?'

Jesse in the meantime had been dealing responsibly with their breakup, managing his feelings like a pro, and out on casual dates every few weeks, having the life of Riley.

'Yeah, George, defo. See you after work at Café Pana.'

Georgia couldn't keep her feelings hidden anymore, and divulged everything that had been happening to her. Tears streamed down her face, as she sat in full view of everyone at the café.

'I never realised George. You are breaking my heart with that news. Do you want to go somewhere where we can chat in private? People can probably see you crying here.'

'Screw them, I couldn't give a shite. Tears are just another human emotion. Jesus, what is it about laughter that it's allowed and praised, but when we cry, we feel ashamed, and worried we are making others uncomfortable? Well, newsflash people, life is uncomfortable sometimes. How often do you see a girl or guy crying in the street for that matter? Almost never. Crying is a human emotion too, just like laughter. It pisses me off, and I'm sick of hiding all the time,' sobbed Georgia.

'You never cared what people thought and you still don't. You are the most liberated person I ever met or will ever meet in my lifetime. Cry your eyes out girl. I'm here for you, and from now on I'm going to go walking with you a few times a week to keep you company. I told you I'll always have your back.'

'Words cannot express how grateful I am Jesse. I know neither of us regret breaking up, but I just gotta get back on my feet, and learn how to be on my own again.'

'I know George, and you will. Allow your family and friends in too, and in time it will get better, I swear.'

He decided to walk her home, and he watched her get out her tins of cat food to feed two stray cats on the window. As he waited, he became aware of three men dressed in yellow hi-vis jackets working on some pipes a few doors down.

'Get your tins out for the lads, for the lads,' he chanted.

Georgia broke down laughing.

'Oh, I needed that laugh. Thanks Jess!

With a promise of seeing her again soon, he left her alone, but in a better mood. Her joy was to be short-lived, as the following morning, the same old fear and anxiety in her was awake and ready for the day, eager to torment her and take her down. She dragged herself up the hill once again to the Abbey, and was informed there was a new module starting that day, the history of classical music. This entailed the class having to listen to music from the dark ages right up to modern times. Recordings of men chanting songs from long ago, and then classical music pieces.

'This music is driving me literally insane,' she complained, to her classmate Brian, a really nice biker dude in his fifties, and rocking long hair.

'Really? I love it. It makes me drift away and feel so relaxed. Pure bliss.'

'I don't know why, I always thought I loved classical music, and that I would teach only that on the piano, but do you know what? I despise it,' said Georgia, sternly.

'Are you not enjoying the course right now Georgia? You seemed so enthused all along but now…'

'No, I'm not enjoying it. Who knows, maybe I will leave soon.'

'Whaat? You can't! You are at level 5 in music theory, a gifted singer, and we all love you. Why on earth?'

'I don't know. I'm just thinking about it, but thanks Brian,' replied Georgia, with tight lips. *Yeah, I do what I want.*

Her moods were up and down. One minute she was a nervous wreck, the next minute crying and curled up in a ball, or then angry as hell. Her mother rang a few days later checking up.

'What's the matter love? You seem fed up?'

'The doc says I have severe anxiety and a panic disorder, and I'm going for counselling now.'

'Where did all this come from? Why didn't you tell us? How long?'

'It's been happening for the last few months. Instead of fighting the world now, I'm fighting my biggest opponent yet Mum.'

'And who is that love?'

'Me, mum,' grumbled Georgia.

'Oh, love, you need to come home, and we'll get the family together and we'll have a bit of a sing song. You could bring your ukulele and lash out some songs. I think it will do you the world of good.'

'Ok, can we make it Sunday because I have counselling this Friday, and I'll want Saturday to relax. Does that suit?

'Perfect. Your father will collect you.'

At this stage, Georgia had got rid of her car, as she felt she didn't need it because now, she was living in the city.

Friday came, and having had a rough week at the college she was eager to see Hanna again.

'Georgia, how was this last week for you? I hope it was kind?'

'Same old story, if I'm honest. Would you mind if I just cry for most of this session?' asked Georgia, looking completely down.

'Of course, this is your time Georgia, and whatever will make you feel better, I support fully.'

'Thanks Hanna, it's just when you are always trying to look as if you've got it together, it gets exhausting. I'm exhausted. I go to college, and then I walk for hours and hours until my feet won't carry me anymore,' explained Georgia, now crying with her hands to her face.

'Of course it's exhausting, no-one can keep that up, especially when you are suffering. I just don't understand why you put that pressure on yourself?'

'Because don't you know life is a game? And I must play the game,' cried Georgia, now bent forward in her chair sobbing uncontrollably.

'But who says it's a game?'

'My dad,' said Georgia, through stifled sobs.

'Ok, well I know what I'm going to give you for home-work this week Georgia,' said Hanna, smiling coyly.

'Homework, dear Lord, I forgot. What's my assign-ment?' asked Georgia, with mock horror.

'I want you to write a few paragraphs on why you feel you have to play the game, and why life is a game. Can you do that for me?'

'Ah…I guess I can'.

The session came to a close at the end of fifty minutes.

'How are you now Georgia? Do you feel even a tiny bit better?'

'Yes, actually, I feel lighter. I'm sorry for crying for most of the session. It must be so draining for you?' said Georgia, looking guilty.

'Oh, Georgia, now you even worry that you are draining me. Listen, this is my job, and I wouldn't do it if I couldn't handle it. You've been coming here for a few weeks now, and my appointments with you are like respite, like a break, even though I'm still working of course.'

'They are? But all I do is complain and cry?'

'Even so, you just have a lovely light presence. You're a very kind girl with a big heart, worried about everyone, even your counsellor,' said Hanna, getting up off her seat and heading for the door.

'Thank you so much for saying that Hanna. You don't know how much you are helping me now, you just don't.'

'Ah, I think I might' smiled Hanna.

'Now, don't forget the homework, see you next Friday.

'Oh yeah, I had forgotten already. I promise. I must go now and walk a million miles haha. Thanks again.'

Sunday beckoned, and Georgia's father, Harry, collected her and brought her home for the day.

'Your mum told me about what's going on George,' said Harry.

'Yeah, I'll be fine.'

While they drove, intrusive thoughts began to flood her brain again.

Open the car door and jump out mid- traffic. It kept repeating on the journey, and Georgia was starting to feel very uncomfortable and shifty.

'Show me your eyes. Hmm, troubled. Hold on kid, this will pass and you'll be your old self again soon. You're from strong stock, do you hear me?' said Harry, smiling.

'God I can never hide from you guys. It's either my eyes or my voice. Ye always bloody well know,' said Georgia, frustrated.

'Of course, we do. We are your parents. We made you and you are an equal split of the two of us. You've got your mother's kind nature, and you've got my strength, feistiness and my dashing good looks. You're lucky your mother didn't marry that old boyfriend of hers, Johnny. Only a face a mother could love,' sniggered Harry.

'But mum's feisty too, and maybe I got her looks?'

'Yeah, true, so you've got a double share of both those things. Aren't you a lucky girl? Look George, when the going gets tough, the tough get going.'

Soon after, they arrived at the house, and Georgia's sister Sophie was there with her three kids, two girls and a boy. Her brother, Oscar arrived a short time later, instruments in hand, ready for the sing song. They were just about to head to the conservatory, when Sophie caught Georgia about to throw back a valium.

'Wait, you don't need that George,' said Sophie gently.

'I do Sophie, my nerves are in tatters.'

'Mum told me, but Georgia, just give it a chance. If you still feel that way in a while you can take one,' said Sophie.

'Ok, sure I have my nuts anyway. I asked the girl in the chemist shop to advise me as to what food would be good for anxiety, and she suggested nuts, so I'm like a squirrel every day now,' laughed Georgia.

They proceeded to go into the conservatory, and everybody took turns to sing a song, and then it was Georgia's turn.

'Right guys, I'm going to do a bit of improv today,' announced Georgia.

'What do you mean love?' asked her mother.

'I'm going to make up a song on the spot with the help of my ukulele.'

She began to pluck on the strings, creating an intro to the song, a song still not born.

'It's called Give Up The Game.'

With that, the words flowed from her very soul....

Short Instrumental plays:

♫

Give Up The Game

When I was a kid, my daddy told me play the game
I said really daddy, why can't I just be me?
I went through my life taking his advice
And now I see it's time for a change
Time to rearrange

Chorus
Put your heart in a box
Put it up on the shelf
Stop making plans
Live for the day

I don't care if anyone likes it
I don't care if I seem different
I'm going to be me
Take it or leave it
I don't give a shite if you don't like it
I'm going to be free
And say what I mean

Give up the game
I'm hanging up my shoes
I'm done being what you want me to be
And I'm free
Give up the game
Oh, you can take it back
I don't care anymore
I'm just me

But the good news
is I'm free
I'm free
I am free as a bird......

♫

Georgia looked up after finishing the song, to notice that the room was completely quiet, and everyone was staring in silent awe.

'That's a hit right there,' reacted her sister, shocked and excited all at once.

Her father and brother nodded profusely in agreement.

'It is George, how did you do that?' gasped her father.

'I don't know, it just flowed from me. It was quite fun, I must say, I surprised myself,' giggled Georgia. 'Now, a hit lads, come on, as if?' said Georgia, looking sceptical.

'We are going to meet every Sunday from now on,' said her Mum.

Everyone agreed.

'What else is going to fly out of you, my special girl?'

'I don't know Mum. Judging from the way I'm feeling right now, anything could come out of me. There's a storm brewing in my soul at the moment, and maybe I can get creative with it, and use it to my advantage. Beauty in the dark Oscar.'

'You got it sis. You can be the yellow rose if you want to.'

'Something to think about.'

The whole experience had lifted Georgia, and she felt that even if it should all wear off the following morning, at this moment in time, she was just grateful to be happy. The feeling lasted for two days, and sure enough, her worst enemy, anxiety, returned to pay her a visit just in case she had forgotten her. It was Wednesday now, and she was sitting in class with the same old horrible familiar feelings and symptoms.

I hate you anxiety, you bastard. I have to give you a name. What will I call you? She wracked her brain to think of someone she hated, and how she could use that name for anxiety. *I have it. Yes, I will call you Kate, the girl who pushed me to leave school. She was a bully and was constantly trying to bring me down, even though I never allowed her to win. That's your name now Anxiety- Kate. A worthy name for a worthy asshole like yourself,* she stormed inside her head.

'Georgia, it's time for your piano lesson,' called Bradley, her piano teacher, interrupting her brainstorm.

'Oh, yeah. I'll just get my piano sheets Bradley. I'll be there in a minute,' muttered Georgia, suddenly flustered after being dragged away from her thoughts abruptly by Bradley.

She walked into the piano room and sat down next to her teacher.

'Ok, play me the scales first,' he commanded.

She ran down through the scales with success.

'Good, now have you been practising your piece for the upcoming exam? It's only three weeks away now,' he said, looking as strict as ever.

'Am, I've done a little practice,' she replied sheepishly.

Bradley knew they had a schedule to keep, or she wouldn't pass her level 2 piano exam. He had his own pressures as a teacher and had to meet his own targets. Sometimes that meant playing hardball with the students, and he was sensing that maybe Georgia hadn't been trying hard lately.

'A little? You know how important this is, and I don't mess around,' he barked.

'Yeah, look. I'll just start. It will be fine,' said Georgia, looking unsure.

She placed her shaking hands on the piano keys, and proceeded to make multiple mistakes on the piece she was supposed to have perfected by now.

'Just stop Georgia, what the hell? You just made a ton of mistakes. You need to get your head in the game girl, and what is it with the shaky hands?' he grumbled, grabbing her piano piece sheet and crumpling it a little with temper. 'Start again,' he ordered, handing her back her wrinkled up sheet.

In a fit of temper, she looked at him in fury, and grabbed the piano sheet, crushed it into a ball, and threw it across the room.

'What in the name of God has gotten into you Georgia?' he asked, flabbergasted at her behaviour, as she had always been so polite, and was always an excellent student.

'Well, you wrinkled the paper, so I finished the job for you. It's gone across the room now, and there it will stay,' said Georgia, defiantly.

Bradley's face turned from temper to softness.

'Is there something bothering you? You never act like this. Forget everything I said and just tell me what's the matter with you?' he said, knowing he had to change tact.

'Ok, my hands are shaking, and I can't do the piece because I have severe anxiety at the moment. I'm fed up and I refuse to do piano class. I'm going to start digging my heels in around here,' explained Georgia, with eyes that let Bradley know how upset and frustrated she was.

'Oh, I never knew, you should have said before. How long has this been going on?'

'A few months.'

'Sit down and tell me about it. I'm actually a teddy bear when I need to be,' he said, tapping the empty seat she had just vacated.

When she analysed his face, she just knew she could trust him, so she opened up, and let him in on all the gory details. Bradley was being completely supportive and understanding, and Georgia was seeing him in a whole new light. At that moment, in her mind, he was now a legend.

'Now, I hope you feel better after our little talk, but we must do some work as well today. I know you can't play piano, but do you have any songs that you wrote lately and maybe we can work on them? Sid told me you sang one of your own songs in the room downstairs.'

'That was a secret, the little fecker. As it happens, I wrote a song last Sunday at my parent's house when we were having a sing song. Actually, I didn't write it. It was improv, composed on the spot with the help of my uku-lele.'

She was now brightening up with the idea of not having to do a proper lesson with Bradley, and potentially having fun for a change.

'Right, have you got a copy on your phone that I can listen to,' he asked, interested.

'Yeah, I do, I'll play it for you now.'

She played the song and watched Bradley hum along. He began to fiddle with the piano keys for a few minutes while Georgia watched him.

'Right, I think I have it. Will you sing it for me and I'll play along on the piano?' he asked, ready to do what he was gifted at.

'Whoa, that was amazing, what a thrill. I can hear it in a movie. Can you?' he said, amazed.

'Firstly, I never realised what a gifted piano player you are. You're a genius. The way you played my song just blew my mind. I'm just marvelling at how you did that, and secondly oh my God, you say, you can hear it in a movie! That would be other-worldly!' shrieked Georgia, now feeling as if she had reached the stars, she was so high. 'Thank you from the bottom of my heart for the chat, and for playing my song. You've given me hope. I feel as if before this, I was walking on a dark lonely street, and now it's as if somebody turned on all the streetlights at once, and I'm so high on life right now. I don't know how long it will last, but who cares right now. You have given me something to focus on.'

'I'm over the moon for you Georgia, it was my pleasure. Now our time is up, but hey that was damn fun, so it was, and remember before you go, you've got a hit there and I think it belongs in a movie.'

'Thank you soo much Bradley. There have been times I wanted to throw you out of that window, but not anymore,' laughed Georgia, heading to the door while viewing Bradley as if he was a saint.

'I'm lucky I'm on the right side of you then,' he laughed.

Georgia spent the next two days unable to concentrate on anything other than the experience in the piano room with her teacher.

It was magical. I cannot wait to tell Hanna. 'I'll tell her that I did my homework assignment, but it's not on paper. It's in a song, and I'm freaking out with joy right now.

While she walked for miles, Georgia would listen over and over on her phone to the version of her song she had recorded with Bradley. On Friday afternoon, she practically skipped into the city centre, ready for her appointment with Hanna. She waited patiently in the waiting room for Hanna to greet her, as she always did.

'Hello, Georgia, lovely to see you as always. Come on in,' directed Hanna.

Georgia took her usual green seat across from Hanna.

'Georgia, you look really bright and happy today and it's wonderful to see you like this. Have you got some good news to share with me?' asked Hanna, curious as to the change she was noticing in Georgia.

'Yes, Hanna, I do. I'm really high right now, and not on drugs. High on life, and I can't get back down from the clouds,' explained Georgia, grinning from ear to ear.

'Oh, my, how great to hear. What has happened?'

'Do you remember that homework you gave me, about playing games?'

'I do indeed, did you do it?'

'I did, but I did it in a song. I just made it up on the spot the other day at my parent's house. Anyway, on Wednesday my piano teacher put music to it, and he thinks it belongs in a movie, and that it could be a hit. My family think so aswell.'

'That's amazing. I'm so thrilled for you. Can I hear it?' asked Hanna, enthusiastically. 'Absolutely, it's my home-work sure.'

She took out her phone, and put it on the floor be-tween herself and Hanna. Georgia watched as Hanna went into full concentration mode, listening eagerly to the song. When the song finished, Hanna looked dumbfounded at Georgia.

'I know you told me you were at music college, but I didn't know you sang. What a powerful voice you have. I agree with your teacher and family. That has to be a hit right there. It just has to be.'

'Do you really think so?'

'I definitely do. It's excellent. I must hear it again. This is a really special unique experience for me because in all my years of counselling, no client has ever given me their homework in a song. It's just so different and unique.

What a wonderful way to express yourself. Was it a cathartic experience for you?'

'Really, nobody ever did this? That's so cool. I live for uniqueness, and I feel really proud and encouraged by that, and thank you for accepting the homework in a different way. I majorly appreciate it. To answer your question, yes it was very healing for me. I feel lighter for it, getting out all those emotions through song. I find myself a bit scared too though. If it's a hit, could I handle all the attention? I don't know. People don't realise it, but I'm shy underneath all the bravado, and don't court attention in my life,' said Georgia, looking more serious at the thought.

'Oh, you are an interesting complex character Georgia. So many layers. I have never met anyone quite like you. Just remember, don't be afraid. We have all these sessions to thrash it all out. There's plenty of time. Don't rush anything but just enjoy the moment. I wonder too about the words in the song, are they true? Are you ready to give up the game?'

'That's a good question. If I'm to be honest, I think deep down in my soul, that is what I want, and I'll try so hard, but I've been this way for a long time, and I'm sure it will take time to break these behaviours, even if they are bad for me.'

'That is good enough for now, the intention is there, and these things are a process. One step at a time. As they say Rome wasn't built in a day.'

'Yeah, it wasn't,' replied Georgia, looking pensive.

They both continued to chat for the session, and Hanna decided to keep things light and breezy for the remainder of it, as she was eager to support the lift in Georgia's mood.

All too soon, Sunday dawned, and it was time for another sing song at her parent's home. She looked at her ukulele and threw it over her shoulder.

My new best bud, my little magical instrument. The improv won't work without you. What will you gift me with today?

17

…Managed to put Georgia back together again

Just like clockwork, another song was born. Much as Georgia was delighted to be coming up with new material, she realised that her emotions were very raw, and these songs were a reflection of the angst and inner turmoil she was experiencing. When the following Friday arrived, and she met with Hanna, her demeanour had changed from the last session.

'You seem different today.'

'Yeah, I'm feeling very raw at the moment. I came up with another song last Sunday.'

'That's great. Are you going to play it for me?'

'Yes, I'd love to thanks Hanna. I'm realising that creating these songs is like purging all of my feelings, and I'm wondering if these songs can be my homework each week from now on?'

'Absolutely, I see how hard you are working on yourself Georgia, and really you need to slow down a little. The songs can be your homework because I believe they are helping to heal you.'

'Thanks for your understanding. They are helping to heal me, but they are making me very emotional too. This might sound strange, but I'd like to play you this song and cry my eyes out as we listen. Is that ok?'

'Of course, you are unearthing very deep stuff right now, and you are bound to be very emotional. Remember this is a safe space right now, and you can cry your heart out. It's ok, I promise you.'

'Thank you, Hanna. The name of this song is 'Let It Roar.'

With that Georgia took out her phone and placed it between herself and Hanna and played the song, and Hanna watched as she bent over in the chair and sobbed her heart out.

Short Instrumental:

♫

Let It Roar

I'm sorry folks if I'm a bit brash
If I'm a little bit cranky
I am sorry
I have to speak my mind
I have to free my mind
I have to say what's in my heart
and do what's right for me

Chorus
Oh, I'm sorry baby
Oh, I do try
but I gotta look after me
By speaking up now

Speaking up now
Speaking up now baby
And letting the lion roar

Let it roar
And it'll get quieter then
It won't need to roar
Let it roar
Let it come out
And it'll get quieter then
It won't need to roar anymore

Anymore
Anymore
Anymore

♫

'That really is such a stellar song. I can hear all of the pain and hurt in your voice, and I understand the raw emotions that are in you right now. Is there more than anxiety going on I wonder. Are you thinking of your ex-boyfriend in that song?'

'Thank you so much for saying that. I'm not thinking of my ex actually. There's a man called Alfie, whom I fell in love with, but it's a long story. He was from Galway and he has moved back there now. I realise that I can't afford the luxury of thinking about him at this point. I have to focus my efforts solely on getting better. He does creep into my mind, but I just kick him back out, because I can't deal with that at present. I will someday,' said Georgia, sadly.

'I believe you know instinctively what you need to do

right now Georgia, and you're right, we need to focus on getting you back up and running again, and then we can talk about him, whenever you like.'

They continued to talk for the session, and each week the same process would continue. Georgia would come to her session with a new song and cry her heart out at it. Therapy was becoming second nature to her, and she began to look forward to it at the end of every week. Unfortunately, back in the college, the same old demons were rearing their ugly heads. She was realising that in spite of the therapy, the healthy eating she had now adopted, and the miles she was walking every day, she just wasn't cutting it. She had now stopped smoking weed which she had smoked regularly over the previous number of years, cut down on the cigarettes, switched to decaf coffee and given up booze. It was a Friday and she went to see her vocal teacher Maya.

'Hey, Georgia, what are you going to sing for me today?' asked Maya brightly.

'I'm not going to sing today Maya. Can we just talk?'

'Yeah, of course, what's up?' asked Maya, looking bewildered.

'I've been dealing with severe anxiety since June, and I've been going for counselling all these months. I know it's only September now, and it is working. It's helping me a lot but after deep reflection, I realise I just need time out.'

'Time out? For how long?'

'Like permanent time out. I need to get myself better fully and just concentrate on that.'

'I'm shocked hearing that Georgia. You've blown me out of the water, and it's really strange, because I'm thinking of packing up and going back to London myself,' confided Maya.

'Really? But you are so amazing at your job, now I'm the one blown away.'

'I guess we are in the same boat actually, only my problem isn't anxiety. I just miss life in London, and my family and friends. I'm so lonely here. I don't know what to do. My brain hurts from thinking about it all the time,' said Maya, looking frustrated.

'Will you come out with me to the smoking area on a non-official smoke break? We need to talk,' said Georgia.

'Go on, ya bad thing. Let's do it,' replied Maya, with a naughty smile.

They both went out and huddled in a corner, and Georgia looked to Maya.

'Maya, I want to help you with your dilemma if I can.'

'I'd love it, please do,' replied Maya, looking interested.

'Ok, here it goes, life is like a train. The train is going on a journey, just like life is a journey. Sometimes, the train stops at a destination and we are meant to get off there. Sometimes, it stops somewhere else that isn't meant for us, so we don't get off at that stop. Some passengers come on, as in friends and colleagues. Some passengers get off, and it's because they have nothing more to teach us. Some passengers we don't ever want to get off the train, and some passengers we throw off because they are bad for us. Some passengers are new to us because we never met before, but they're there to teach us something new.'

'Right, this is interesting. I like this analogy. Carry on,' replied Maya, soaking up every word.

'Ok, now you're at a destination at the moment. It's this music college in Cork, and you love the people and the job, but you're deeply unhappy inside, missing home, so what good is the job? You can get an amazing job in the UK also. Yes, you will miss us passengers and we will miss you. I say leave this destination, get on the train again and travel to the destination of the UK. Wave goodbye to all the passengers on the train, and thank them for their contributions to your life. Does it all make sense?'

'It makes perfect sense. Thank you so much Georgia. I'm getting on the train, and I'm picking my old destination, home. It all makes sense now. But what about you?'

'Well, I'm getting off the train for a while, and I'm going to rest from my journey on the side of the tracks, and lay my head down for a while. When I'm better, I will take a new train, and meet some old passengers, and some new. I don't know where the new destination will be, but it will be exciting to find out.'

'You say that so calmly.'

'Yeah, because right now I am calm. Underneath this storm lies the real me. I'm just fighting to get out from under all that smothering. I will get out. It will take time, but I'm a fighter, always have been, always will be. Right now, anxiety has the upper hand, but it won't stay that way,' said Georgia, with a steely glare.

'We can do this Georgia, we will rise up through the shit, we will,' said Maya, convinced.

'I'll never forget you. I'll carry you in my heart,' said Georgia.

'It's been an honour knowing you. I'll be waiting to see what you do next.

'And, you also. Two of us against the world.'

The bond was sealed, and Georgia walked back into her class, and waited for the right moment to announce her upcoming departure. This time was going to be tougher than ever, because the music college had become her second home, and the students like members of her family. She got back to class, and waited until it was 1.25 pm, five minutes before the end of school for the day.

'Guys, can I say something?' asked Georgia, standing up.

'Yes, of course,' said Lewis, her teacher, looking confused.

'Thanks Lewis, I have a little announcement to make. I have some personal stuff I'm dealing with at the moment, stuff I don't want to discuss right now. I love this music course, you Lewis, and you guys, but I have to leave. I'm finishing today.'

'But, Georgia, no!' piped up Ben, shocked, and then the others joined in.

'Ye are all wonderful and I wish ye the best. I hope to see you all down the road. Thank you for everything. Now, I'm terrible at goodbyes, and I'm trying to keep a stiff upper lip here, so goodbye,' said Georgia, looking calm and definite.

She looked around her to see the different faces of her friends, looking sad and shocked. It was a look she had seen before in her life many times. This time there would be no tears. It was time to get better and get her power back. She knew if she hugged anyone or addressed the issue any further, she would breakdown, so she grabbed her bag and headed for the door. Before going through the door, she stopped and looked back with a smile.

She hurried down the stairs and headed for home before anybody had a chance to catch up with her. When she got home, she continued to hold back her tears, and save them up for her counselling session later that day, so she arrived in Hanna's office in the afternoon to cry a river.

That evening her mother phoned to be met with a completely devastated Georgia.

'I've left the course Mum. I've never said this before, but it's time to be honest. I'm a God damn failure. I look back on my whole life, and I couldn't stick to anything. I've been trying my hardest for so long, and even when I get back to my old self, I think it's time for me to take time off from trying. I'm all out of ideas' said Georgia, in between sobs.

'Georgia, you're not a failure. Ok, so you've never been able to hold down a job and maybe you have failed in that regard, but at the end of the day, does that matter?'

'I don't know Mum.'

'No, it doesn't George. What matters is the kind of person you are. That's the legacy you leave behind. You're loved by all your family and everyone you meet. You have a special loving kind way about you, and you're always trying to help. Look at how you love all the animals, the children and people in general. That's so much more important, can't you see?'

'Maybe,' said Georgia, cheering up.

'Now, listen to me, you are down right now, but you won't stay down, and you know that.'

'Yeah, I'm just having a moment, you know?'

'You are like the oak tree.'

'The oak tree? How so?'

'Oh, my girl. The Oak tree is one of the most loved trees in the world. It's the king of the forest and it symbolises strength. It might grow slowly, but it's doing it at its own rate. The storms and hurricanes of the planet fail to knock it down. They might shake it to its roots, but they fail to knock it down. You remind me of the Oak tree because you're still standing tall, in spite of all the knocks and disappointments life has thrown at you.'

'Oh, I absolutely love it. Thank you so much Mum. Yeah, I'm still standing. You're right. It's not the failures that matter, it's the trying, and I have been God damn trying. It's the getting back up, and I'm going to get back up Mum. I don't know how long it's going to take, but God damn it, I'm going to get back up and stay up,' promised Georgia, with total conviction in her voice.

'Watch out world, bitch will be coming back, bigger than ever.'

'That's my girl.'

Georgia lay awake that night, wracking her brain as to what she could do to help herself further, and decided she needed to educate herself on anxiety. She needed to get to know her enemy, every single part of her. The following day, she went to the library, joined up and took some books on the subject back home with her. She also started to download books online. She figured without the music course now, she had even more time on her hands, so she began to read all day, every day, and as evening approached, she would go outside and walk for hours as usual. She was only marginally meeting friends, as she was so focused on educating herself. Through her research, she found a meditation app called Breathe. It was a male speaker, and his voice instantly calmed her. She began to listen to all of the recordings on the app, and started to practice meditation daily. Within a few days, after daily meditating, she could feel the difference entirely, and through this app she learned about mindfulness and breathing. Her crazy moods were now beginning to steady, and the beast was beginning to quieten. She was learning that with mindfulness, and by just being in the present, she could escape the intrusive thoughts, and for months she tried everything she could to do just that.

In the shower in the morning, she would focus on the water and the soap, and the feeling of the hot water touching her skin. When she got dressed, she focused on each action. When she washed the dishes, she mindfully washed them. She would read, focusing on every word, never letting her mind wander, and she knew at this point from her reading that everybody's mind likes to wander, but she just kept bringing it back to the moment she was in. She was now learning about Thich Nhat Hann, a Vietnamese monk, who promoted mindfulness and peace all over the world. She would hold his words in her mind as she walked, 'Peace is every step.' It was a gigantic effort for her every day to engage with mindfulness in every single action and task, but to spare herself from intrusive thoughts and anxiety, she did it over and over. Everything else in Georgia's life had taken a back seat at this point. Her weekly schedule consisted of reading, walking, eating healthily, meeting up with Jesse a couple of times a week, going for her counselling on Fridays, and to her parent's house on Sundays to make more music.

Her counsellor watched Georgia over the months get stronger and stronger, and she continued to be her greatest lifeline throughout the process. Her brother Oscar was also engaging in meditation and mindfulness, and was more versed in it than Georgia. They arranged to meet to discuss it all. While at a café in town, Georgia was excited to tell Oscar all she had learned, and how she was using mindfulness as a major tool in her daily life. Oscar took in all the information first, and then said he wanted to add his thoughts.

'I think it's incredible what you're doing George, and I really admire it, but I see flaws that can be ironed out here.'

'Right, what exactly?'

'It seems like you are hiding behind mindfulness, to escape from your anxiety and thoughts, punishing yourself if your mind wanders. To keep this up every day is a pressure. You have to embrace it gently. The experts say to think of it like a feather rubbing off a glass, gentle, not jerking back and forward between thoughts and mindfulness, and not punishing yourself for thinking. The brain wants to think all day, that is natural. You have to ease your way back gently from thoughts into the present because the real beauty lies in the moment.'

'Ok. I have been jerking between the two definitely. It's like my mind wanders and I drag it back fast, for fear I will think and have intrusive thoughts again.'

'For this to work, you have to believe in it, not use it as a form of escapism. For example, if a parent is always distracted, and their child is trying to show them a picture they drew, or share some news, if that parent is mindful, they will see it. They will enjoy that moment and be present with it instead of missing it. They know that the child will grow up one day, and that these are precious moments.'

'Yes, ok, give me more examples.'

'Ok, if you are walking anywhere, say the park and you are in your head, you can't smell the flowers and appreciate nature or how the sky looks that day.'

'Yeah, I want to feel those things. I want to see them fully because I adore nature.'

'If you're in the shower, you can feel the hot water on your skin, and feel thankful that you have hot water, unlike some people in the world who don't even have a shower or running water. Gratefulness is a huge part of this George. When you meet people, you notice some people have no attention span, and they are not even listening to you after twenty seconds. When you are mindful, that's not the case. You are present, and you're concentrating on what they are saying, and giving them the gift of listening. Do you understand?'

'I do fully, and I agree. Most people are bad listeners and they're interested only in themselves. I don't want to be one of them.'

'That's it exactly. We don't know how long we are going to live and don't you want to feel the present with all its experiences? When you kiss somebody, you feel the kiss in its entirety. The same goes for a hug or a touch. That my sis, is mindfulness. Seeing the beauty of it, and how it absolutely transforms your life, not hiding behind it, to escape anxiety. The Buddhas teach you to sit with whatever you are feeling, and not to run from it. To be comfortable with the uncomfortable, and then watch it leave. The mind is a transient thing and it will never stay somewhere for long. Your moods will be changing all day. You will move in and out of different states constantly, and just move with them, like water. Water stops for nothing. It cuts through everything, the rocks, everything. It keeps flowing. Be like water.'

'You're a bloody genius you are. This conversation for me is like a new awakening. I've been doing it all wrong and looking at it the wrong way altogether. I get it now though. I really do.'

'I will take no credit whatsoever, because all of these teachings have been passed down by all the wise Buddhas and teachers out there. All I have done is pass on their words. I'm delighted if I have helped by doing that.'

'Helped me? You just changed my life bro. I've just realised something else now too.'

'Yeah, what's that?'

'I've been calling anxiety by the name of Kate, as you know, after that little rotter I went to school with. Fighting Kate is like fighting myself, and I won't do that anymore. I'm renaming Kate now to Mate. That's her new name. I'm going to make peace with her in my mind, and with anyone else that has ever been nasty to me. I forgive her and all of them, and I don't do it for them. I do it for me, because I need peace now Oscar.'

'Mate, that's brilliant. I'm so proud of you sis, I really am.'

'Yeah, I'm suddenly asking myself, what was I meant to learn from all this? What was it trying to teach me?'

'What did you come up with?'

'I'd have to think it over, but right now, I feel I'm a nicer person for it. I'm completely empathic towards people's struggles now, more than ever before. I'm more forgiving. I realise that I've hit rock bottom, and that the only way is up. I'm human and I have a vulnerable side, and I need to be ok with that, and I've learned that I can handle anything, if I just get up and try,' said Georgia, with a tear in her eye

'That's so sweet George. Now are you still flipping those intrusive thoughts?'

'Yeah, I am, that's bloody hard work too, I'll tell ya.'

'Your next goal now is to let them move through you and watch them leave. You will be a dab hand at this yet.'

'Yeah, Hanna, my counsellor has been trying in vain to help me with that, and my meditation app suggests that constantly too. All in good time Oscar.'

'One step at a time. Just don't forget there's no cure for anxiety George. It's part of the human condition. Everybody feels anxiety at one time or another. It's about management. You just manage it, and you can do that through meditation, mindfulness, healthy eating etc., and just accepting it as part of you. Make friends with it as you said.'

'Absolutely, from now on, when I get up in the morning, I'll ask Mate if she would like to have breakfast with me, and do some reading, and maybe we could go for a walk together. My good ole Mate haha.'

'That's it, ask Mate if she would like to hang around with you all day if she wants, and what you will realise is that when you do that, she will leave pretty quickly.'

'Yeah, she will be on her way to make mates with somebody else,' chuckled Georgia.

'She's a busy girl in fairness. She has paid me a nice few visits as well, bless her sweet heart,' howled Oscar.

'Such a thoughtful guy or girl, not sure,' laughed Georgia.

They continued to laugh, and enjoy the mutual sarcasm, and their shared love of it all. Oscar had learned all of this information to help himself, and his clients, and knew the power behind it. He wondered should he approach the topic of autism with Georgia again, but instinctively knew that she had not mentioned it in counselling or she would have told him. She had her own battles to deal with already, without adding autism to the mix, so he stayed quiet about it. He would bide his time, and figured one day she would be ready, and he would be there to catch her when she was.

Over the next few months, Georgia would wake up each morning, and have her usual coffee and cigarette. She would feel the familiar growl of anxiety, and then she would remember her chat with Oscar.

Oh yeah, hey mate. Do you want to have coffee with me? How great to have your company. What shall we do together today? Maybe we should meet some of our friends, she would laugh to herself. Mate was visiting less and less, especially during meditation. Georgia still had her head in her books on anxiety every day, but was now squeezing in time for friends, and starting to laugh again, and relax. She was becoming herself again, coming full circle, just like her mother had promised her, and she was doing it without medication, although she would still carry the valium in her bag every day, just for emergencies. Knowing it was there was enough.

18

Bending with the wind

At this point Georgia had been getting counselling for a year, and as usual on Friday, Georgia visited her counsellor once again. She sat there in the now so familiar little office, looking at the posters on mental health as she waited for Hanna. They didn't upset her as much now, but the classical music that played still had the ability to irritate the hell out of her. She wondered to herself if she would ever like classical music again, and figured that it had just attached itself to a dark time in her life, and was just guilty by association possibly.

'Hello, Georgia. Great to see you. Come on in. You look happy today.'

'Hi, Hanna, yeah, I'm feeling good. Sure as you know, I've been doing good lately.'

'You sure have. The hard work has been paying off. Any new developments for me?'

'Yeah, some great ones. In the last week, I've been letting the intrusive thoughts move through me, without battle or flipping them. You will be very proud of me,' said Georgia, chuffed with herself.

'Oh, that is absolutely wonderful. I'm beyond proud. What changed?'

'It took me a year to be fair, but last week, I just tried to be brave, and I said to myself, these are stress hormones, and maybe I will have them for the rest of my life. If I stop fighting them, maybe they will leave, but for some reason, they need to pass through me, and if I put up roadblocks every day it's not helping. I am not my thoughts, or so the Buddhas say. Last week, I lay back on the couch, and relaxed my body, and said out loudly, go on, pass through. I don't fear you anymore. You have no power over me. You are just a culmination of built-up stress, fear and anxiety. Maybe you are the child in me, who is afraid, my subconscious, I don't know.'

'That's it, you met them with kindness, and you are being gentle with yourself. That is a major development. You have arrived Georgia. Welcome back to the world,' said Hanna, lighting up with joy and pride that she had done her job well. 'Have you got a song for me this week. Homework?'

'Ah sure, of course I do haha. It's called 'Give Her Room. I wrote it for my sister, well I improvised as usual. She has been a wonderful support to me. My entire family has. My friends, you, everyone. You've all been a great help. Ye all collectively got me to where I am now.'

'You did all the work, it's no good without that. We can't do the work for you, and you did it. I'm not sure I 've ever seen someone who worked so hard to get better. You're a fighter. Ok, now let's hear that song.'

Georgia placed the phone between them as she had done so many times.

'Love the song, what a wonderful sister you must have. You're not crying though?'

'Thank you. That means a lot. No, there are no tears left to cry. I think the well has run dry, thank God.'

'I see, I also find it interesting that this is the first song that's about recognising pain in someone else rather than being focused on your own.

'Yes, I understand now that everyone is going through their own pain and I'm feeling strong enough now to see that's just part of living.'

'That's very wise, and what about the song 'Give Up The Game? Are you going to pursue it? Everybody including me, has said it's a hit.'

'I'm going to let that simmer for a while, because of the attention it may bring. I'm not ready for that. I may never be, if the song were to become a hit.'

'Speaking of that song, I don't wish to be inappropriate, but if you don't mind, I would like to dedicate that to you Hanna. You're the reason I wrote it, and I just want it to be a nod towards you for all you have done for me. I'm just so grateful. Would that be ok?'

'What a gorgeous gesture. Thank you so much. I would be honoured. Nobody has ever dedicated a song to me before.'

'Thank you for accepting. When I get the song recorded, I'll send you a copy, but I just don't know if I'll ever release it.'

'That would be amazing,' said Hanna, touched by the gesture. 'Now this is a lovely moment and I don't want to spoil it, but I have something to share with you Georgia,' said Hanna, looking serious.

'Wow, should I be worried?'

'Not at all. You've come a long way, and I've watched you get back on your feet. I've been waiting for the right moment to break this news to you.'

'The right moment for what?' asked Georgia, looking worried and confused.

'I've been offered a job, working with troubled teens back in Lithuania. It's something I really want to do. I know this will come as a big shock to you, and I'm so sorry about that. We have built a terrific working relationship here, and I know you rely on these sessions so much. I'm torn inside about the effects of this on you, and on my other clients,' explained Hanna, looking sad and guilty.

'Oh, I wasn't expecting that for a moment. I don't know what I was expecting. This is a huge shock, but you picked a good time. I'm strong now and back on my feet. Hanna, you are an angel sent down from above. I want only good for you. God knows you earned it. I want you to be happy, and I just want to let you know, I'm fine with this. I completely understand and wish you every bit of luck and happiness in the world,' said Georgia, trying her best to keep a stiff upper lip, and not cry.

'Thank you so much for understanding Georgia. I'll miss you as my client. You are wonderful, and this has been such a unique experience with you, and I treasure it as your counsellor. I don't want you to stop your sessions. I can give you the name of this other counsellor. She's amazing and she can continue on with you. I really think you will get on with her.'

'Thank you and I do appreciate it. I'll take the name, but maybe it's time for this little bird to fly the nest now.'

'But we still have room for a few sessions. We have a few weeks left, and we don't want that bird to fly prematurely.'

189

'I do understand, but I have to be honest. I just want to rip off the plaster now, and deal with the sting. If I get into trouble again, I'll have that name of this other counsellor which you are giving me. I promise I'll use it, but my heart just tells me now, that this has to be our last session, and I just want to take life to the next level. I hope you understand. This is how I have to deal with it,' said Georgia, still holding her composure.

'Of course, I understand. I see by you now that you are trying to be strong, and you don't want me to feel guilty by showing emotion. It's true isn't it?'

'Yeah, you're right. You're holding enough guilt without me adding to it. I want to be strong for you right now, and not make you feel badly, because you don't deserve that.'

'If you want to help me Georgia, you will do what comes naturally. Cry your eyes out right now if you want. I feel like doing it myself.'

'Are you sure? I can hold it.'

'Please feel what you are feeling right now,' said Hanna, sadly.

With that Georgia broke down completely, and sobbed and sobbed bent over on the chair. Ten minutes passed and she eventually stopped.

'I guess that well wasn't dry after all God damn it,' laughed Georgia.

'You are only human Georgia.'

'I know. I feel badly for crying but thanks. I need to go now. When I get that cd, I'll send it onto you.'

'But we still have time Georgia. You're only halfway through your session.'

'Don't worry about that. Have a coffee for the other half, and a short break before your next client. I need to say goodbye now. Words can't express my gratefulness. I only pray that you realise what you have done for me, and how amazing you are. Thank you, and may the sun light the path you walk on, and shine on everything you do. May you be well and your loved ones well. Your presence makes a difference in this world. It counts as you do. When you sleep at night, know that please. You're not one of the zombies out there looking out for number one. You're an angel. Goodbye Hanna. I won't hug you as that would be inappropriate.'

'That means the world to me and everything you said, I won't forget. Never change Georgia, never change,' said Hanna, with tears in her eyes, now shaking Georgia's hand.

'I won't. I hope the good you do, returns to you. I hope every tiny grain of it finds its way back to you,' said Georgia, now heading for the door.

She kept walking and didn't look back. She couldn't wait to get home, and crumble for a while, as she processed the shock of saying goodbye to Hanna for the last time. With a heavy heart she walked slowly, feeling the breeze on her face, and watched the trees as they swayed. People were passing by going about their business, and she continued as if in a trance.

You're on your own again girl, but you've got this. You can handle anything. All good things come to an end, and I've just got to learn to bend with the wind.

Over the next few days, Georgia began to think about her next move, and after much deliberation realised she had no idea what to do next. She knew she had to take a break from the music for a while. In her mind, the whole thing had gone a little sour. She wasn't ready to delve back into the course, but she was happy to continue writing songs each week. She figured there might come a day when she would want to use them, but right now she had no clue what she should do next in terms of her career. Deep inside, she understood that if she started something, she would probably fail again. It had to be a time out, and she had learned from her meditation app, that the best ideas come when you don't actively think about them. Apparently, the brain is a problem-solving machine, and all the answers would come to her in their own time, so she waited and waited.

She spent the next year, engaging fully with her meditation, mindfulness, reading and walking. She would meet friends and family, and life became normal again. The panic attacks had stopped, and the intrusive thoughts were decreasing rapidly. She was now able to take them in her stride and let them flow through her, and not be bothered by them. She had also discovered after countless tests that the visual disturbances she was experiencing were harmless ocular migraines, which in turn brought great relief. Bit by bit she was trying to piece her life back together. She searched for a new house, and in December she found a cosy one-bedroom house with a garden in the suburbs. It was a lovely, peaceful place where she could relax and feel at home. Leaving the stray cats behind her broke her heart, but she knew her neighbour would look after them. She realised for the sake of her mental health she had to get away from all the anti-social behaviour in the neighbourhood. It was time for a fresh start.

Living in the new house changed everything. She was now able to focus, and manage her anxiety. Another six months passed, and in this time, she changed from reading books on anxiety and self-help to romance fiction novels.

She now walked for hours because she enjoyed it, rather than trying to distract herself from her anxiety. While she walked, she could now enjoy nature and engage in mindfulness. This time was about finding herself and gaining some peace. She found a new interest in health and fitness, and she was doing this five times a week to improve her mental and physical health. She had energy to burn from the moment she woke up, and she kept herself active from morning until night. It was a happy time in her life, and she treated it like a vacation, always planning that she would find her purpose again once she felt she had fully recovered. Once her brain fog lifted, she began to think about Alfie again. She had blocked him out for a long time, and now she realised that roughly two years had gone by since she'd left the Abbey.

Now that she had allowed herself to think about Alfie once again, she was thinking of him night and day. Instead of feeling troubled by it, she enjoyed the fantasy of maybe seeing him again, and how down the road, their paths might cross again. She had no contact details for him, and he had no social media profiles, but his face had burnt itself into her memory, as did the treasured moments they shared. She had stayed single since the Alexandre fiasco, choosing not even to go on a date. She needed to know that she could be on her own. It was her greatest challenge, but in her heart she felt Alfie was the one, and yes if she tried hard enough, she knew she could track him down, but she was a proud, stubborn woman. Could she really risk hearing him tell her that she had blown it? In her heart, she feared he would. It was easier to fantasise that destiny would bring them back together sometime in the future. She wondered what he would think of her now, as she felt she had changed. Her wicked sense of humour was more alive than ever, and she was still adventurous and feisty, but having survived the storm, she was, in ways, an entirely different person to the one who had entered it. She had found the courage to discard the mask and had vowed to own her feelings, but would she have the courage to share her true feelings with Alfie?

19

What's behind door number four?

The following spring, Georgia was taking an early morning stroll near her home, and admiring nature when she remembered the chat about Autism that she had with Oscar some time previously. She realised that she had never discussed that possibility with Hanna during her counselling sessions, nor had she discussed Alfie. They had been far too busy focusing on her main problem of anxiety. Something within her knew that now was the right time to explore it, and she felt strong enough to cope with whatever diagnosis she would get. She knew the curiosity would get the better of her. She just had to know, but deep down she believed that Oscar was wrong, and that she was not autistic. She made an appointment with her doctor asking him for a referral. He gave her a number for an expert in the field, but when she rang, this guy was too busy to take any more appointments, so she rang her brother Oscar to talk it over.

'Hey, Oscar, do you remember what you said a few years back about thinking I was on the autistic spectrum?'

'Yeah of course. Have you been thinking of following it up?' asked Oscar, surprised.

'Yes, actually. I'm feeling very much together, strong,

and calm, and have done so for a while. I feel now, I need to know the truth. I've put it to the back of my mind for long enough, and maybe it could answer a lot of questions, and explain why I've found holding down a job so hard over the years.'

'Absolutely, I mean we don't really know until you see a professional psychologist, but I would feel very confident about my assumptions. Do you believe you are autistic?'

'Well, I don't really, but a little part of me says maybe. It's hard to see that in yourself. I mean, if you had never mentioned this to me, it certainly would never have dawned on me in my entire life, that's for sure.'

'Would you think about sharing it with the family before you get tested?'

'I'll tell them for sure. I think they will be quite surprised to hear it though.'

They talked about it some more and a few days later, while having a family get together, Georgia brought up the subject with them. They felt the same as Georgia. They reckoned in so many ways she was very capable, but acknowledged that holding down a job was something she failed to do, no matter how hard she tried. Everybody was happy for Georgia to go for an assessment, so Oscar went to work ringing around professionals, trying to find the perfect person, somebody he knew would handle her gently.

After a lot of research, Oscar found an expert in the field in Dublin. Her name was Sarah and her office was in the city centre. Georgia made her first appointment and as she found the building, she noticed the number four gold plate on the blue door.

There's no going back now. She pressed the bell and was led into a waiting room. It was a modest size and an average building. Sarah came out from her office and welcomed her.

'Come on in Georgia. I'm Sarah. It's a pleasure to meet you.'

Georgia studied her. She was small, curvy with brown hair, about forty, and she had a kind, friendly and inviting face.

Ok, I like how she looks. She seems nice. Good.

'It's lovely to meet you too, thanks for seeing me.'

'Of course, you've come from Cork today. That was a bit of a journey.'

'Yeah, and I'm really proud of myself, because normally I have no sense of direction and get lost easily, but I made it here, yay.'

'So, you think you might be autistic?'

'My brother thinks I am. He's a psychologist, and he has studied this area in depth. I personally don't think I am, but I'm open to finding out the truth.'

They went on to discuss Georgia's life, and when she explained about her work history, she began to cry with the guilt of it all. When she finally gathered herself a few minutes later, Sarah asked her if she ever took information literally.

'Yes, I do, all my life, but not every single time. We have a running joke about it in the family. I remember when I was a young teenager watching a film with my family, and my sister mentioned that the actor in the movie had a chip on his shoulder. I told her the next morning, that I had spent the entire night looking for the actor's chipped shoulder, as if a piece was missing, and I couldn't find it. My sister was inconsolable, and we still laugh at it today,' said Georgia, brightening up with the thought.

'You have such a fun way about you. That's an amusing story and it's so good that you can laugh at it. Are there other examples?'

'Ah, it happens constantly. I miss a lot of jokes and innuendos. One day, a man asked me for a light for his cigarette. I gave it to him, and he said thanks, and lit it. He then scrunched up his mouth and said that the cigarette was actually disgusting. I was bemused, but realised soon after he was just kidding. It happens most of the time, but other times, I'm quick to get the hidden meaning. It's weird. It's my default to take things literally, I guess. My brain seems to need that extra few moments to process. I have millions of stories like this. I believe I'm very intelligent, but there are certain things where you just say what the hell is up with me? Also, I can't build anything, not even a kinder egg toy. Any presents I ever bought for my nieces and nephews, they had to build themselves. A lot of elementary tasks are beyond me, but then I'm great with the more important ones.'

'This is really helpful Georgia, thank you so much for being so forthcoming.'

The session lasted two hours, and Georgia gave every bit of information she could think of. If she were going to do this, she would have to be completely transparent. Sarah explained to her, that she would have to fill in a lot of paperwork at home over the coming weeks, and that a family member would also have to write about her childhood and behaviours. There would have to be another session later with her and a family member. She filled out all the paperwork, asked her mother to fill out her side of things, and posted them off to Sarah in a timely fashion. Then after careful consideration, she decided she wanted Oscar to be the person who accompanied her to the final interview.

On the drive up to Dublin, Oscar and herself treated the day as a road trip, and they were both excited to bring things to the next level. Her parents and siblings were on the phone, wishing her good luck whatever the result would be, and telling her that nothing would change. Deep down, Georgia felt that it would be a negative result anyway, but at least she would know for sure. After a two and a half hour journey, Georgia and Oscar arrived at Sarah's clinic. Through their emails and their previous appointment, Georgia had really taken to Sarah and was over the moon with Oscar's choice of psychologist.

Georgia learned a great deal from her meeting with Sarah who explained that Georgia had spent much of her life coping with sensory issues which often left her feeling exhausted and overwhelmed. Sarah explained that interactions with other people often resulted in sensory over load for Georgia leaving her drained and in need of quiet, downtime away from others in order to replenish her energy stores and re-regulate her senses. She also discussed Georgia's difficulties with processing some forms of information, explaining gently that her mind was simply wired a little more creatively than her peers. It was evident to Sarah that Georgia hyper-focused on many different things, to the point of exhaustion. Three hours later, and after careful review, and consultation with Oscar, they realised that Georgia and Oscar were in complete sync as to how they viewed Georgia's experiences from the time she was a child to the present moment.

'It's quite amazing how you both agree on everything. Sometimes, people have a very different memory of things, even when they are from the same family,' said Sarah, surprised.

'I swore to myself, I would give you the entire truth, and I'm probably hanging myself out to dry here, calling out all of my eccentricities, but we need an accurate result. I'd say I'm digging my own grave,' laughed Georgia.

She had managed to keep her composure up to this point, but now it was beginning to wane.

'Do you think I could get the result today? Our appointment is nearly up, and it would mean the world to me, but I understand if you need more time,' said Georgia, eager to get the result if possible.

'As it happens, I can do that, because in this case, I have all the information that I need.

'Oh, that's amazing, thank you Sarah. Ok, I'm ready,' said Georgia, bracing herself.

Sarah stalled, and after what seemed like the longest pause gently turned to Georgia.

'Georgia, what result do you think it will be? And what result do you want it to be?' asked Sarah, with a serious expression.

Oscar sat quietly observing.

'Well, that's easy. I think it will be negative and truthfully that is what I want, even though it would mean not having any explanations for the struggles I've gone through in my life. I still want it to be negative,' said Georgia, eagerly.

'Well, Georgia, I'm afraid that I can't give you that answer. As you know we test scrupulously, and you've been completely honest and transparent, and I admire you so much for that courage, but I would diagnose you as a Level 1 autistic person. It's the category where you might describe one as having mild autism, and generally people in this category would require little in the way of supports.

Sarah went on to explain people with a Level 2 and 3 diagnosis require significantly more support in managing their day to day life. At Level 1, many would call this Asperger's Syndrome, a high functioning autism, but the medical field does not use that term anymore, however, many autistic people continue to use it as they feel they relate to that more.

Are you ok?' asked Sarah, sympathetically.

Georgia began to break down crying.

'I'm gutted if I'm honest. Shocked and gutted. I didn't expect it,' said Georgia, in between sobs.

Sarah drew her chair close to Georgia.

'Watch what I will draw, and look at these circles. Do you see all the different parts? Family, career, interests, talents etc. Now look at the small circle in the middle. That is autism. That's just a part of you. It's not all of you. You have many layers, and this is only one layer, and why does it have to be bad? Autism can be a great thing. You will often find people with it are extremely caring, and loving towards people, and towards animals. They can be highly intelligent and super creative. There are many greats in the world who are autistic. No two autistic people are the same though. You have more than excellent communication skills, but where you mainly struggle is you are highly sensory. Your senses become overwhelmed and you need to shut down for a while. That is why you have such problems with holding down a job. You also have problems remembering things, and you need to rely on lists a lot of the time. Sometimes, you need to take more time to process information. In so many ways you have remarkable talents and I must tell you, I have met people who were gutted to find out they weren't autistic.'

'Really, what? Who would want that?'

'They would have liked to get answers and explanations, and instead they were left mystified. In your case now, you have answers. You can make this a positive thing. You seem like such a polite, caring, good person and the letters your mum wrote about you brought a tear to my eye. Similar to the way your brother spoke about you today. This is a shock, I know, but I just pray you will come to understand that it doesn't have to be a bad thing. It can be a great thing.'

'But all my life I felt I could do anything, be anything. Now, suddenly it feels as if there's a glass ceiling,' said Georgia, tearfully.

'Forget about the glass ceiling, to hell with that. There's no glass ceiling but there is clarity. In time, you can understand your strengths and areas of difficulty, and you can work with them. You should be unbelievably proud that you have come this far, and you've received no concessions your whole life. You've had to observe and learn so much harder than anybody else to fit in with social norms.'

'I suppose life has always been so hard, but it was my normal. I knew nothing else. I observed what I thought made up a good person, like good listening, being kind etc. and I emulated that, and tried to create my character around it.'

'Maybe it's time to stop trying too hard to please everybody, doing what you think is expected of you, and learn about *your* needs, and people should respect that.'

'I am this way for so long, I don't know if I could be any other way now. I've a lot to think about, but I'm a positive girl who needs to live in the sunshine, not the dark, and Sarah I will rise up through the shit. By God, I will, I always do. I'll figure this out,' said Georgia, with conviction.

'I've no doubt. I'll send you lots of literature and recommendations, and a breakdown of this whole process, listing your strengths and difficulties, and I'm here if you have any questions, anything. I'm here for you.'

'Thank you so much Sarah for everything. You were my dream person to deal with in this process. I'm so grateful for that. You are truly amazing at your job and have just been incredible. I'm truly thankful to you, and for all your efforts and words of encouragement. I will turn this around. I've just found all of this out. You'll see. I'll find the positive in this and make you proud yet,' said Georgia, now cheering up.

'Georgia, it has been an absolute pleasure. Everything your mum and brother said about you is true. You're a special lady, and I look forward to hearing how you're getting on in the future.'

Oscar thanked Sarah for looking after his sister, and they walked to the car together. They were only in the car five minutes when her mum rang.

'Well, did you find out the result today? I'm dying here waiting to find out. I timed your appointment, and hoped I called at the right time. Thank God I got you.'

'I'll just put you on speaker so Oscar can hear you Mum.'

'Well, your daughter is autistic. I'm Level 1, the mildest form. Aren't you the lucky one?' joked Georgia, reviving her sense of humour.

'Oh, that's fantastic! Congratulations,' said Jo.

'Congratulations, my God. You would swear I just won a prize. You're hilarious Mum,' giggled Georgia.

'I mean it love, we're so proud of you and now you have answers. That's worth gold. You can stop beating yourself up now, and be bloody well proud of how hard you've worked all your life, with no help,' said Jo, full of pride.

Her father Harry and her siblings were cheering in the background.

'Well done George, ya bloody legend.'

'Thanks guys, this is the weirdest experience ever. It's actually turning out to be hilarious and you know me, I love to laugh, but guys this is my secret. I know ye know, and I'll tell Jesse and a couple of close friends, but that's it. It's under lock and key. Don't tell the kids. I don't want them changing their opinion of me, and I don't want people to put me in a box. I'll be carrying on as normal, and it's nobody's business but mine.'

'Of course, we won't tell a soul, if that's what you want.'

They finished the call, and on the journey back to Cork, Georgia and Oscar chatted away about the session and the day.

'I couldn't have done it without you bro. You were right all along, you clever clogs.'

'I'm just so honoured you trusted me, and brought me to the session. I'm just beyond proud to have you as my sister. You've no idea how happy I am for you.'

When Georgia finally got home, she threw herself on the couch, consuming all the information of the day, looking up videos and everything she could find on the topic. She had been doing plenty of research in the run-up to the final appointment, and felt like she knew all she needed to know, but it was different now, she had been diagnosed. It was real. A few days later, she had an epiphany and rang her mother.

'Mum, I've been doing some thinking and I've realised, I don't give a bloody shite who knows I have autism, not a shite. I never cared what people thought, why should I start now? What have I to be ashamed of? I'm a good person who has been trying her best all her life, and if I'm to hide away in shame, that just keeps the stigma of autism alive. Tell whoever you like. I want to do my part to help this community shout loudly and proudly, and teach the kids of today to speak up and be counted. The world will never change otherwise, and I want to be part of that change. I want my nieces and nephews to celebrate difference, and never be afraid of anything.'

'I just don't want you rushing anything George. The appointment was only a few days ago. Maybe you're having mixed feelings about it, and you'll change your mind yet. I don't want you feeling exposed and having regrets,' pressed Jo, concerned Georgia was being impulsive.

'Mum, I've always known my own mind. I know what I'm doing. I won't change it. I'm not going to get on Facebook and announce it or anything, but when it comes up at the right time with people, and I think it fits, then I will say it. I don't have to run up the street shouting it from the rooftops, but I'm ok with everybody knowing.'

'Ok, no problem then. I think it's a marvellous attitude.'

Georgia proceeded to ring Jesse to tell him her news.

'I'm a bit surprised by the news of course, but I think it changes nothing to be honest. You're just you. You've always been quirky, but that's part of your charm. I think you will find that generally people will feel the same as I do,' said Jesse, warmly.

'Yeah, maybe so, and if they don't embrace it, that's their issue, not mine. I won't be taking it on board. I'll be just living my life and doing my thang. I know now that I'm highly sensory, and can only be with people for a certain time limit. It might be two hours or eight hours, I don't know. I just know when my senses become over-whelmed, I have to leave.'

'But how will you explain that to people?'

'I think I'll just tell them that I'm like Cinderella. When the clock strikes midnight, my glass slipper falls off, and I've to return home, and play with my little mouse friends again hahaha,' howled Georgia.

She listened while Jesse broke down laughing on the other side of the phone.

'Keep that shit up,' chuckled Jesse.

'I fully intend to, don't you worry,' replied Georgia, still giggling.

She had found her humour, and it was bigger than ever. For the next month, she didn't engage in any research regarding autism. Quite frankly, she was bored of reading about it. She needed something new to occupy her.

It is what it is, but what if I could use it to my advantage? What if I could unlock some hidden potential? What if I wrote a book? I always wanted to try my hand as a writer, and my parents have said so many times that I have a unique turn of phrase, and would make a great writer, but what would I write about?... Maybe anxiety or children's books. She decided to let it sit in her mind for a while, and promised herself she would revisit it again soon. She carried on with her fitness regime at home, and decided to paint the house, and transform the garden. She was on fire, and her energy was soaring. She was aware she was hyper-focusing again, but at least she understood it this time.

20

'Life tried to crush her, but only succeeded in creating a diamond.'

One evening while surfing the net, she stumbled across an interview with a female author who had written a romance novel. The story grabbed Georgia's attention, so determined to buy the book, she took herself off to the nearby shopping centre, only to be told it was sold out. She went back home and decided to get the audiobook online. While lying back on the couch, and listening to the story, she decided there and then she would fulfil a lifelong ambition of hers to write her own book. It was a spur of the moment decision, and she had no idea what she would write about, but surprisingly now the answer was clear. It could be a romance fiction novel loosely based on her own life. She figured she could write all about Alfie, He was on her mind day and night, and just as she had led an interesting life, she felt that his life could also be material for a good story, or at least she hoped it would.

She took out her phone, and downloaded a writing app, and so her book was born. Hours later, she realised she had clocked up thousands of words, which just flowed from her like a river. For the next couple of days, her brain behaved in a way it never had before. It went into complete overdrive, and from morning until night, thousands of ideas flooded her mind and onto her pages, as if her life depended on them. She had opened a door that had never been opened before, and an avalanche of ideas was unleashed. After hours and hours of relentless writing, she ended up feeling drained, uneasy and upset. She stared in the mirror and saw a weak, pale figure looking back at her. Writing about some of her own experiences was bringing up ugly memories of her past, and she wondered if she could handle it, but resolved to keep trying.

Over the next few days, her brain continued to process all her thoughts, but at a slower rate, and soon the raw feelings had passed. It was all madness, but now she was beginning to realise that her brain had been very kind giving her the entire story so quickly, and that she was privileged. Then out of the blues, her father Harry rang her.

'How are you today?' asked Harry.

'Guess what? I'm writing a book. I've always wanted to do it and now seems like the perfect time.'

'That's an excellent idea. You always had a fantastic way with words. Your mother and I always felt that one day you could be a great writer. What kind of book will it be?'

'It's a romance fiction novel, loosely based on my own life, and it's all written already in my head. I just have to get it onto the pages now. It will probably take me a year I'd say.'

'Written already, you even have an ending in mind?'

'My brain just went into overdrive and I figured out the whole story. I won't lie. It freaked me out at first, but now I'm thrilled because it just flows like a dream onto the pages.'

'You don't have a computer though George. Are you writing it manually?'

'I'm writing it on my phone, and when it's finished I'll go to the Internet café and edit it, then send a copy to a copy editor. I'll take it from there,' said Georgia, nonchalantly.

'When can we read it?'

'Ah, it would only bore ye guys. It's a romance novel. Ye wouldn't be interested.'

'We would of course. Sure, my favourite books are by Jackie Collins. I can read a romance novel and really enjoy it. Send on whatever you have,' said Harry, eagerly.

'Alright then, I'll send you on a few pages, and I look forward to your opinion,' said Georgia, excited to have her first readers.

She emailed on the first two chapters without delay, and the following day her father rang her.

'Well Georgia, your mother and I read those chapters and we think you're gifted. You were born to write. Keep going and don't dare stop,' said Harry, over the moon.

'Really, yay!!! I'm so thrilled to get the encouragement. I do believe in myself and the book, but it's amazing to hear that, and I hope everybody feels the same. I don't know what the title will be yet, but the book will be a mixture of dark and light, and be true to life.

Two days later, there was a knock on the door, and there stood Georgia's parents with a box in their hands.

'What the hell is that? You know it upsets me to receive gifts,' said Georgia, nervously.

'A writer needs a laptop, and this is a present from us. Now, go write up a storm and show the world what you can do George,' said her mother.

'Ah lads, this is so expensive. How can you tell I will finish the book? I have quit so many things in the past,' said Georgia, feeling guilty.

'Let's just say we know you'll finish it, and it will be a great success. You have a story to share, one which could help others to understand themselves better, and live in harmony with their struggles.

'Thanks guys from the bottom of my heart. Now, I can work at a faster pace.'

She continued to write every single day, for hours on end. She wrote about Alfie and their love story, but changed his name and some details of their friendship. She was careful not to give too much away. She wondered if he would ever see or read her book. Writing about Alfie helped Georgia channel all the feelings she had for him, and it helped her reminisce about their time together, and the wonderful memories she had of him. In her mind, he may never read these words, but at least she would chronicle them on paper, and release herself from them.

Over the months, she received constant encouragement from her family and friends, and her mother and father took it in turns to read the chapters to each other. Time passed by, and she poured her heart and soul into the book, always focusing on quality instead of quantity. She would dream of the day her book would be published. Her wish was that whoever would read it, boy or girl, would be entertained, feel happy and sad, and maybe change just a little for the better for reading it. She looked on it as her little gift to the world, in short, her legacy. She had never had children to keep her memory alive, but maybe she could live on through her book. She would continue to write no matter what. Nothing was going to get in her way.

This time she would finish what she started. This book was going to be her last attempt at being a success. The game was up after this. She decided to include the songs she had written in her book. They were part of the story, and they needed to be there. Everything had a purpose, and that purpose had to be played out piece by piece, right up to the end. Four months later, Georgia rang her mother Jo.

'You won't believe it. I've done it. I've just written my last page,' said Georgia, sounding tired but happy.

'I can't believe it. I thought you said it would take a year.'

'You will laugh now Mum, but I wrote it with gusto because I was afraid I might die before the story was finished. Now I can die happy hahaha.'

'You crazy girl. I can't wait to read the end. I know it's going to be unique like the story so far.'

'Oh, I hope you love it Mum. This book is all that I am, and all that I have,' said Georgia, with conviction.

'I know it is love, it's so evident in your writing. I know you've given it your blood, sweat and tears, believe me, and it will pay off,' said Jo, convinced.

'I hope you are right Mum. This is my last attempt at being a success. I swear to Christ. I've nothing left, and I'm done looking for more ideas. I give up after this. I know you've never heard me say that before, but I mean it. I give up if this doesn't work. I'll take my beating graceful as a swan, but this is it. I'll just get on with my life, and never dream of success again.

'You're already a success George. You just can't see it, but I hope one day you will. Now, get off the phone so your dad and I can read the end.'

'Ok, ok. Go for it. Let me know what you think asap.'

At twelve o' clock that night, Georgia's phone rang, and it was Jo to say how much they had enjoyed the ending. The first draft of the book had been completed in only four months but it ended up taking the remainder of the year to re-draft and edit it, so that it was ready to send to the publishers. Soon, everything was ready to go, and with all her files at the ready, she researched all the publishers in Ireland and the UK.

I'll go further if I have to. I'll knock shamelessly on every door to get one of them to sign me up, and take on my book. Determination was ripping through her body and soul. It was Saturday morning, and she got out of bed, made her breakfast, and with her trusted coffee and cigarette in hand, she sent her first copy of the book to one of the biggest Irish publishers she could find, Milford & Lyons. She knew she would have to be patient as replies came slowly. This was going to take months possibly, but she was on a mission once again, and felt it would take what it would take.

The next few weeks passed, and on a Thursday morning about 10 am, while Georgia was having a lie-in, her phone rang. She noticed it wasn't one of her usual numbers. She was still half asleep, but curiosity got the better of her, and she swiped the screen on her phone to answer the call.

'Hello,' she said sleepily.

'Good morning, is that Georgia?' asked a well-spoken voice.

'It sure is,' replied Georgia, relaxed.

'Georgia. I'm so glad I got you. My name is Siobhan, and I'm ringing you from Milford & Lyons Book Publishing House in Dublin.'

'Oh, goodness me. What a surprise. Thank you so much for getting back to me. Did you receive my email then?' asked Georgia, now fully awake and shaking with excitement.'

'Haha! Did we what? My co-editor Jillian has dark circles under her eyes because of you.

'I'm hoping that means what I think it means?' said Georgia, thrilled out of her mind, now sitting up on her bed and lighting a cigarette to calm her nerves.

'Yes, it does. Jillian came across your book yesterday morning, and she's been reading it ever since. She told me she got two hours sleep as she had to finish the story. Actually, I myself am hoping to read it this evening, and I can't wait after her glowing recommendation. We would both love to meet you. Are you free next Monday and can you come to Dublin to our offices?' asked Siobhan, eagerly.

'That's perfect. I'll be there and thank you so much again.'

For Georgia, it was like winning the lotto. She was wildly excited and she didn't know if her feet would touch the ground again. There was no turning back now. Over the next few months, Siobhan and her staff got to work getting the book ready for promotion and distribution. The book hit the Irish market and before long Georgia found herself doing book signings and promotional events up and down the country. Georgia was living the dream but each night as she lay down, she would tell herself, that she'd be happy to give it all up if only she could have Alfie back. Night and day, she continued to think about him, and wondered if he ever thought about her. She figured he was probably living in Galway doing his Marine Science course, absorbed in his own life, and totally removed from what was happening in hers.

21

Chasing the ghost of her

Just as Georgia had predicted, Alfie had been working hard on his degree in Marine Science back in Galway. He had never returned to Cork since the day he left, and said goodbye to Georgia. He figured it would be too painful. She had broken his heart, and he felt he just had to move on without her. Much as he tried, he had never forgotten her. Almost every day and night, she would drift through his mind, haunting him. He would often dream as he slept that they had met again, and were together, but then he would wake to the cold, harsh reality, that it was just his imagination playing tricks with him.

Over time, he had learned to live with the lodger in his mind, just like Margot had warned him. He knew he had felt love, but it was only the unrequited kind. Nevertheless, she was there in his heart, no matter what he did to shut her out. At times, he would lay in bed, and leave his curtains open, so that he could look up at the moon and stars, and pondered on how they both shared the same sky, her in Cork, and him in Galway. He wondered if she ever thought about him, the way he did about her. He would revisit every meeting they had, minute by minute, thinking about the way she looked at him, and spoke to him. He remembered every detail, and analysed whether he had bailed out on her too quickly. She had looked so troubled when he told her he was leaving for Galway. He had been so abrupt. He wondered if he had hung on, could they have ended up together eventually.

He had cut contact with everybody in Cork, so he had no way of knowing where she was or what she was doing. *Whose arms is she sleeping in tonight? Who holds her hand and drinks coffee with her in the morning? Who dries her tears when she's sad? Whose jokes does she laugh at, and who shares her bed? If only it was me,* he dreamed. He knew if he created a social media profile, he could track her down, but then felt he would probably be met with rejection, just like before. He carried on going to college, and did his best to focus on his studies, and despite the distraction, managed to get excellent marks. The lecturers noticed him, and told him, that he would have no problem in getting work when the course ended. They could see his determination, motivation, and commitment.

Over the last couple of years, he had gone on a few dates, but the longest relationship had lasted six months. He found himself looking for traits of Georgia in these women, even in the tiniest of ways. If he found just one attribute in them that reminded him of her, then he had gained something, but it never happened. None of these women was Georgia, because there was only one of her. At times, as he headed into the city on the bus or his bike, he would scan the crowds looking for her, even though he knew that was impossible. She lived in Cork, and she would have no business in Galway, but still he kept on looking. Sometimes, he would see a woman with long blonde hair, and wearing similar clothes to Georgia, and his heart would beat faster only to learn a few seconds later, it wasn't her. It was never her. He did his best to get on with his life, partaking in sing songs with his old group in O'Flaherty's where he worked before the music course. As he sang the songs, he thought of her. Some evenings, he would take a break from study, and play his guitar in the sitting room in front of the fire. His father Paddy, would listen to him singing his own compositions.

'What's that song son? It sounds like a love song you made up,' asked Paddy, one night.

'Ah nothing,' replied Alfie.

'It doesn't sound like nothing. Has a wee lass stolen your heart? You can't fool me son. Who is she?'

'Ok, it's a song about a girl I met in Cork. I fell in love with her, but she went off with another guy.'

'Why didn't you mention it before? You left that course a few years ago now.'

'I've never mentioned it to anybody back in Galway. What was the point? It never came to be.'

'And you are still thinking about her all this time? I know you've been on dates but nothing ever seems to come from it!'

'Margot told me a few years ago, if you fall in love, you'll know for sure when the person becomes a lodger in your mind. Well, this girl is a permanent lodger. I gave her the eviction notice several times, but she won't leave. I've given up trying. I'm haunted by her.'

'But that's no way to live son. I thought you were happy all this time.'

'I'm happy Pops, but not in my love life,' said Alfie, sadly.

'Ah son, this is a disaster, but who am I to talk? I think of your mother every day and night too. I kiss her picture every night before I go to sleep, and dream of her. It looks like we are both haunted now. You know I never wanted that for you son, and that's why I told you when you were growing up to forget about women.'

'I tried Pops, but that's like asking me not to breathe. She got in there, and I just live with it now.'

'But if that's the way you feel, why don't you do something about it?'

'Sure, how could I? She is probably married with kids now. A woman like her would be snapped up in no time. It's pointless. I'm sure someone else will come along one day to take her place, God I hope so.'

'To be honest, you said she went off with somebody else, and that's not a glowing recommendation. I suppose we all want what we can't have.'

'It's not like that Pops. She's my dream woman. She's special, beautiful, unique and kind. I could go on all day. We all have some cross to bear, and she's mine I guess, but don't worry about it,' said Alfie, dismissively.

'Is that song you wrote about her then?'

'Yeah. It just helps to release the feelings inside.'

'Start from the beginning and let me hear the whole story,' said Paddy, sitting down on the sofa.

'I always love to hear my son sing.'

With the fire burning brightly in front of them, Alfie began to play his guitar and sing his own song about Georgia.

'Wait. What is the name of the song?'

'The ghost of you.'

'Righto, pretty fitting then, carry on.'

♫

The Ghost Of You

I was fine till you came along
singing your song
Oh, what a song it was
I looked in your eyes
and saw my future
You were the B for beautiful
B for beautiful

Chorus

You played with my heart
And turned me upside down
Left me with nothing
but the haunted dream of you
I look for you everywhere I go
But they're not you, oh no

All we do is share the same ol' sky
The moon is mine and it is yours
Come back to me come back to me
And give me your love
Give me your love

I won't need to pretend that you are mine
can't keep this going all the time
Will you be mine
Will you be mine
And give me your love
Give me your love

Can't keep this going all the time
Just pretending you are mine

♫

'That was lovely son, but I can hear the pain in your voice as you sang. Now I'm going to take a nap here but carry on singing.'

Alfie continued to sing for another hour while his father snored on the couch, and eventually he got a blanket and put it over him and headed off to bed himself. The following morning, he returned to his rented one bed apartment in the city, where he actually spent very little time, because he enjoyed being at home with his father. Time passed by, and his course finished. Soon he would get his results, and meanwhile he decided to go back to working in his old bar job for the summer.

On a very windy day in the middle of June, Alfie had time off, so he went for a stroll through the city. As he walked, he tried to light a cigarette, but the wind repeatedly blew out the flame.

Oh, for God's sake, feck off wind, he thought to himself irritated. He was passing by a shop and decided to take shelter while he tried again to light his cigarette. Something caught his eye in the window. Georgia Harte, her name was written on a book. The cover showed a girl drawing a love heart on a window. *Jesus Christ! Am I in the twilight zone right now?* He took a step back, cigarette in hand, and looked up at the name of the shop. It was Moran's bookshop. He had never noticed it in the past. He knew he must have passed it a million times, but this time was different. It was a slightly run-down book shop. The kind that said Old Ireland, and there was nothing modern about it. A red canopy hung over the window, which itself was dusty, and looked as if it hadn't been cleaned in years. He gazed at the book in disbelief.

It couldn't be her. There must be another Georgia Harte out there. She can't be the only one. She never mentioned she was a writer, but that book cover. It's just like that love heart she drew on the café window where I worked in Cork. He felt butterflies in his stomach, and his heart began to speed up with excitement. Everything in him told him to open the door, and go inside. As he opened it, a little bell rang to alert the shop keeper that a customer had entered.

'Hello lad. Windy out there for a summer's day isn't it?' said the shop keeper.

'God, yeah, I was trying to light a cigarette for about ten minutes,' said Alfie, now a little breathless and nervous.

'You should give them up.'

'I know sure, and I will,' said Alfie, now heading for the window to get a closer look at the book.

The title was in red and it said 'The Singer Not The Song.'

'How can I help you anyway? Are you looking for a book in the window?'

'Yeah, please do. There's a book here 'The Singer Not the Song' and I'm wondering about it,' said Alfie, eagerly.

'Ah, yes that's one of our best sellers, it's flying off the shelves. She's a new writer that has entered the scene, and there's a lot of talk about her right now in the literary world. It's a romance novel, not your kind of thing I would say,' said the shopkeeper, now coming out from behind the counter to join Alfie at the window.

'I knew a girl with that name, and I'm curious to find out if it's the same one. Is there a picture of her on the book? I can't see with all the other books stacked up against it.'

'Really, you think you might know her? Wow! I know she's from Cork anyway. The window is a little messy, and I know it's hard to reach it. This is my last copy. Just give me a minute and I'll get it for you,' said the shopkeeper, reaching his hand out to grab the book.

'Here we are, yes, there's a picture on the back. Fine looking woman too isn't she? Is she the girl you know?'

He handed the book to Alfie and there she was in the picture, looking like time hadn't touched her. Still as stunning as ever. Her long blonde hair with soft curls framed her face, and she was wearing a royal blue polo neck.

'Jesus, that is her! I can't believe it,' said Alfie, completely excited.

'How on earth do you know her?'

'We went to music college together. Have you read the book?'

'Ah, I see. No, I haven't. I prefer a good crime novel.'

Alfie fumbled his hands in his pockets, checking to see if he had enough cash on him to buy it, as he had left his bank card at home.

'I don't normally sell the display copy, but I'll be getting a delivery in a few days, and sure go on. I'll sell it to you, seeing that you know the girl.'

'Well, I appreciate that.'

He purchased the book and breezed out the door, and when he got outside, he wondered where he would go to read it.

My place or pops. He decided he would read it at home in his father's house. It was quiet and relaxing there, unlike his apartment in the city. He took off on his bike and made his way to his father's house, then sat on the sofa, and took out his book. Before he started to read the book, he stared at her picture over and over for about ten minutes, and examined the cover repeatedly. *Will there be a mention of me in this book? Probably not.*

Day turned to evening, and he was still reading the book. Late that night, he finally finished. As he read, he could feel her energy dancing out of the pages. He felt it was as if she was sitting down beside him, reading it with him. He read about how she had experienced anxiety, and autism, and wondered if they were truth or fiction. Everything in the pages seemed so authentic, but he knew from the synopsis, that the book was loosely based on the author's life. He was captivated and enthralled by every chapter, and marvelled at her ability as a writer. He read what she described as the love of her life, and he recognised different conversations and experiences which they had shared.

She is talking about me. She is definitely. Jesus Christ! She loved me all along. I just never knew it. He felt as if he was in a dream and the whole situation was surreal. *I'll have to read it again in order to wrap my head around all of this. Maybe I'm just kidding myself and letting my imagination run away with me.* He stayed the night at his father's house, and dragged himself to bed at 2 am. He was exhausted from all the excitement, and the following morning, he called in sick to work, to buy himself more time to explore the book. That evening, his father called him from downstairs.

'Alfie, I have dinner ready. Are you coming down?' called his father.

He came down the stairs looking dishevelled and bothered.

'You look like you were dragged through the hedges son, but you don't look sick. I have your favourite shepherds pie for tea.'

Alfie couldn't contain himself and told his father everything.

'But son, maybe you have it all wrong. I don't want to see you set yourself up for a fall.'

'If you read it, you'll understand.'

'Well, give me the book and I'll read it. I want to get to know the woman who has been melting my son's brain for the last couple of years.'

The next day after work, he headed home. He found his father on the porch, book in one hand, and a brandy in the other.

'Good to see you enjoying life. Have you read the book?' asked Alfie.

'Yes, I'm ready to tell you that I think this book is magical, and the girl who wrote it must have a heart of gold. I've only one thing to say to you son, go down to Cork and find her, and bring her home, so that your brothers and I can meet her.

'That's what I was thinking and I'm so glad you agree. I'll get on to Ross and ask him if he is still in contact with her. She was friendly with everybody, including him,' said Alfie, instantly taking out his phone to message Ross.

'That's my boy. Make it happen.'

He started to message Ross and then decided against it. Messaging might take too long, so he rang him instead.

'Hey Ross, long time no hear.'

'Alfie, is that you?' said Ross, shocked.

'It surely is. I'm sorry I've taken so long to contact you. How are you and how's your wife?' asked Alfie, trying to be polite before railroading Ross for information.

'We're both great thanks. How about you? How's that course going? You must be finished now?'

'Everything is great thanks Ross. I did the course and I finished it a few weeks ago. I'm waiting on results now and feeling confident.'

'Great, good on ya boy. Did you just ring for a chat?'

'I was hoping for a little bit of info,' said Alfie, stalling.

'What can I help you with?'

'I came across Georgia's book a few days ago, and this is really embarrassing, but do you remember how I liked her?'

'Yeah, she's an author now. Who would have expected that? I remember you really liked her, and you were very disappointed that night she didn't turn up for your concert. Do you still like her?'

'I never forgot her Ross, and I know you might say this is crazy, but I think the character in her book is based on me, and that she feels the same.' said Alfie, nervously.

'I didn't read her book yet, but I hear it's very popular.'

'Is she still single?'

'Yeah, she's very friendly with some of the lads, and one of them mentioned lately that she's not with anyone.'

'Yes!!!!' said Alfie, punching the air.

'You're a scream Alfie. Why don't you come to Cork and meet her? I hear she does book readings pretty often in the city. I can find out when the next one is on and you can stay with me if you like.'

'Thanks Ross, you're a legend. I want to surprise her, so not a word to anyone please,' begged Alfie.

When Alfie hung up the phone, his mind was consumed with ideas and romantic gestures he could use. He knew from reading her book she was a die-hard romantic, and that the bar was high. An hour later, Ross rang back, and told Alfie that Georgia was due to hold a book reading in Pearson's Hotel in the heart of the city. For the next couple of days, his brain was working overtime, and finally he decided on a plan. He rang the hotel, and got talking to the manageress called Emma, who loved the idea of romance, and was excited and eager to help him execute his plan to surprise her. The book reading was due to be held the following Saturday night, so he got his hair cut and went out and bought a new outfit. He arrived at Pearson's Hotel, bringing along his guitar as he knew how much she loved music. There he met with Emma, and they went over the plans once again to make sure nothing could go wrong. Georgia was due to arrive at 7 pm for the book reading which was scheduled to last for precisely one hour. Emma told him they were expecting a big audience as the tickets had been sold out for the event. She led him into a little back room, which was next to the Conference suite where the reading was due to take place. He watched as Georgia entered, book in hand, smiling as she greeted everyone on her way up to the stage.

She wore a green dress with black, sexy high heels. The dress fitted her body perfectly, highlighting her curves and swaying out at her hips. As he fixated on her, his heart was pounding with excitement. Forty-five minutes passed, while Georgia answered questions, signed books and proceeded to read some chosen passages. At this stage, Emma beckoned Alfie to take a seat at the back of the room where Georgia couldn't see him. He checked his watch, and it was now 7.55 pm. Time to make his presence felt.

It was showtime, so as Georgia finished the session with a passage from her book describing the cherry blossom scene, he began to strum his guitar softly. For a few moments, she was unaware of the music, but then lightly and gently, the notes of a familiar song drifted in her direction. Surprised, she stopped reading and looked around the room.

'Who can tell me where this beautiful music is coming from?' asked Georgia.

Everybody turned in the direction of the music, which by now was getting louder and louder as he played the intro to 'A Rainy Night In Soho' by Shane McGowan. Georgia looked confused and bewildered, nonetheless, she was smiling as she scanned the room, eager to find the source. At that moment, Alfie stood up so that she could see him. He began to sing the song, while slowly walking towards her. Every note tugged at her heart-strings while precious memories came flooding back. He was now halfway up the aisle, and Georgia stood before him frozen to the spot. Her eyes were wide open in surprise and a smile lit up her face. She forgot her microphone was still hooked to the collar of her dress. She felt like she was in a movie. She ran towards Alfie, threw her arms around his neck, and hugged him tightly.

'So, you know it was you I was writing about?' she asked Alfie in amazement.

'I won't lie. It took me a while. I read the book twice, and it dawned on me that some of those conversations were chats we had on the music course. I remembered them. All the pieces began to fit together. We've lost so much time. I don't want to lose another damn second.'

With that, he cradled her face in his hands, and kissed her like he had never kissed another woman in his life. It felt the same for Georgia. She had never felt such passion in a kiss before. They kissed repeatedly, swaying from left to right with her fingers running through his hair, and him lifting her off the floor with his arms wrapped tightly around her. Oblivious to the audience, they gazed lovingly into each other's eyes.

'Will you be my girl Bee?'

'Oh, I missed you calling me that name so much. I didn't think I'd ever hear it again' said Georgia, beaming.

'Ha, I can tell you now. It never meant bright eyes. It meant B for beautiful, but I couldn't tell you that at the time. I just wanted to call you beautiful every time I met you, so I disguised it. I always hoped I'd get to tell you the real meaning one day,' said Alfie.

'Oh my God Alfie. If I die tomorrow, I'll die happy. I'm on cloud nine right now.'

'Oh, don't go dying on me now. I just found you again. We've only just started. I'm never letting you go again, no matter what games you play Beautiful,' said Alfie, full of love.

'I'm done with games Alfie. I love you. I always have,' said Georgia, her eyes sparkling.

The audience was now clapping loudly and cheering.

'I love you too Bee,' said Alfie, touching her hair and stroking her face. 'I might actually get a good night's sleep tonight without you haunting my dreams. You'll be beside me at last.'

'I absolutely will and as a matter of fact, you've been haunting me too.'

Georgia looked around her to see everyone sharing in this happy moment.

'Is that the fella you wrote about in your book?'

'Oh, I forgot my mic was on. Yes! Let me introduce you to Alfie. I think he has come to sweep me off my feet, and he has certainly succeeded,' said Georgia, now holding Alfie's hand tightly.

The audience was fascinated at this unanticipated and romantic turn of events. The happy ending was enacted right before their very eyes.

Unexpectedly, Alfie swept Georgia off her feet and cradled her in his arms, as if they had just got married. Her laughter echoed through the room, and she waved goodbye to the crowd as they headed for the door. Emma was standing nearby.

'Thank you for everything Emma. I couldn't have done it without you,' said Alfie.

'My pleasure Alfie, that's the best reading we've ever had. Now, go have fun you two,' said the Manageress.

Alfie carried Georgia through the doors of the hotel, and into the crisp night air. Within minutes they were lost in the hustle and bustle of the city streets outside.

22

When all the winding roads lead onto the highway

For once in her life all the planets were aligned in Georgia's favour, and time rolled by, bringing with it all the good the world had to offer. As she sat on her rocking chair in the kitchen, she found herself gazing out on the tranquil scene unfolding before her, in her little garden of dreams. Finally, she had her own Cherry Blossom tree to admire, all day if she so wanted. She would cherish the one month of the year when it bloomed, but found it equally exciting when the pink petals fell like fairy dust onto the grass. She had built a stone arch which led onto her garden and on either side of this, she planted some pink rambling roses. To the right in a sheltered spot sat a special conversation chair, which she and Alfie had found one day while strolling through a garden centre. Alfie had carefully found a romantic spot in the garden for it and placed it beneath a hanging lamp light because he knew how much she loved lanterns. On the warmer evenings, they would sit there and share their news while pondering on the beauty of their magical little garden.

Georgia, as always tuned into everything around her in the present moment. Little birds were flitting from the trees to the nearby bird feeder, while bees and butterflies were enjoying the wild-flowers she had planted along the border. In the distance she could hear the comforting sounds of children's laughter, but these were nowhere as comforting as the pitter-patter of her own son's footsteps as he bounced through the door ahead of Alfie, awakening her from her daydream.

'Mummy, mummy! Guess what daddy promised me?' her four year old son, Jude called out excitedly as he rushed into the kitchen. She looked into his big innocent brown eyes, full of mischief, just like Alfie's and saw in them, the reflection of her own smile. Yes, he looked like his dad but his nature leaned towards Georgia's. In him, she could see her gentleness and her love and concern for nature and animals. She stretched out her arms and pulled him close in an embrace, while her face filled with laughter lines.

'Oh, do tell me all about it, my little man.'

'He said he's going to teach me how to play the guitar.'

Georgia glanced over his shoulder at a grinning Alfie standing in the doorway holding a lunchbox in his hand.

'Did he now? Well, I think that's a fabulous idea. You go Daddy!!'

With that, they could hear a loud thud coming from the hallway. Luigi, their treasured black Labrador came bouncing into the kitchen full of excitement at hearing the sound of Jude's voice and then both the boy and his dog headed out into the garden to play.

Alfie leaned in to kiss Georgia on the forehead and softly placed his hand on her belly.

'How's my Baby Bee and my pretty lady today?'

'Well, Mummy was just relaxing and enjoying her garden when I should have been writing. I must admit that earlier when I was trying to work, she kept interrupting with her little baby kicks. Maybe she was trying to tell me that she liked my story or it could be her little dance to the Eva Cassidy tunes playing in the background. It crossed my mind to call her Belly, short for Isabella. Do you think she would be grateful to us for that?'

'Haha, brilliant. How do you come up with these things? I love it but I don't know if she will love it though,' laughed Alfie.

'So, are we all set for your gang and mine coming to dinner later? Can I do anything?'

'It's all good honey. I'm just ordering a Chinese take-away for all of us. Everybody seems happy with that. No stress and no wash-up,' giggled Georgia.

'That's my girl.'

She watched Alfie go into the sitting room and before long, he was happily strumming his guitar.

'Bring in your ukulele and we'll have our own little session,' he called.

'With this massive tent of a belly, the ukulele would be under my chin,' she answered smiling.

As she walked back to the kitchen, she began to notice the wedding ring on her finger. It was a little tight these days but she wouldn't take it off. It was far too precious and meant the world to her. If it got too tight, they would have to cut it off but she wouldn't part with it otherwise, even if it was only for a while, until this bundle of joy she was carrying saw the light of day. She found herself reminiscing about all that had happened in the last few years. She was now in the middle of writing her third book but at this stage she wrote only for children. The main theme was mindfulness because she knew the powers it held. Her books were full of magical little stories about such things as noticing the wind, the rain, the flowers, the birds and the bees, and the leaves falling from the trees. Over time she had earned herself a decent following and she learned to take her writing career in her stride and to not overwork herself. Alfie was fulfilled in his job as a marine scientist in Cork and they were living comfortably.

She smiled to herself on remembering the time they had travelled to Japan. Alfie had been trying desperately hard to learn the accent to impress Georgia, but instead he was comical every time he tried to pronounce a Japanese word. There was just something about mixing his accent from the west of Ireland with Japanese that had the power to make Georgia laugh so hard, she would attract the attention of passers-by. In fact, he was always making her laugh. It was an art he had developed to relieve her stress and anxiety and bring out the best in her.

Nights on the town, drinks, black coffee and cigarettes had all been replaced for snuggles on the couch in front of a blazing fire, while often times Jude would be sandwiched in between them. Their house was a home of love, warmth, laughter and song. Life was ordinary for them these days but within that ordinary lay the extraordinary. She no longer suffered bouts of dark despair and emptiness. She no longer questioned who she was or where she belonged. She felt safe and loved and knew she was now in the place where she was meant to be.

She remembered the words her dad had often said when he was trying to comfort her. 'It is what it is, my girl and just accept it. This is the hand that fate has dealt you, and always remember what doesn't kill you will make you stronger.' Well, fate had definitely tested her, sending her at times to the brink, but she had always fought her way back. She no longer feared the silence. In her brokenness, Georgia had been forced to sit with her pain and slowly she had put all the pieces back together with a renewed wisdom and kindness which allowed her to feel truly healed from within. Her family and friends had always been there, in the wings, supporting and loving her but only she alone could walk the path in those world-weary brown boots of hers, ducking and diving as life flung lemons in her direction. She managed to climb over each obstacle life placed in her way.

Having autism made her feel different in many ways but it was also a little treasure because it caused her to dig deeper within herself and find her true values. She learned to appreciate what sometimes the eye cannot see but the heart can feel. Her sister had always marvelled that Georgia seemed to see vibrant colours and intricate details that escaped even the most inquisitive eye. She had a wide-eyed and unique way of seeing and understanding the world which remained untainted despite life's trials and tribulations and the passing of time. Writing children's books, particularly for children, who like herself, fell a little outside conventional lines, was a natural transition for Georgia, and one in which she both revelled and excelled. She was happy knowing she could make a difference to many a life through her writing. Deep within her Georgia knew that now she could talk the talk, but she had the added advantage of having walked the walk.

She knew that life could be like a bed of roses sometimes but every rose has its thorns, still with Alfie's hand in hers she felt she could face whatever lay ahead. She didn't realise how quickly the time had passed. Nowadays, she was always busy doing the ordinary and enjoying each moment. That night, as she climbed into bed, Georgia felt a deep sense of gratitude. These past few years with Alfie felt as though life itself had kissed her gently on the head and whispered 'everything's going to be okay now sunshine.' Her early years had been littered with feelings of failure, desperately searching, seeking to belong in all the wrong places and tirelessly moving between courses, colleges and jobs but always unable to stick with any of them for any length of time.

Lying here now in Alfie's arms, his hand gently resting on her tummy, Georgia knew this was where she belonged. She was home at last where she felt secure, loved and needed, safe from the storms that had almost engulfed her. As she gazed out through the window at the night sky, she felt an overwhelming sense of peace and fulfilment and as she cuddled up to Alfie, she silently smiled the smile of a job well done. Georgia fell asleep knowing her whole world, all lay under the same little roof, sleeping soundly under a blanket of stars.

The End

About the Author

Maryjka Miller is a new Irish author who resides in her native Cork city. She lives with her partner of 16 years, Stu and her treasured black cat, Molly. Maryjka is a vegetarian, who sings and writes songs for pleasure, but her main interest lies in writing romance fiction novels. She holds an Honours degree in Social Science (Youth & Community) from University College Cork. Maryjka comes from a very close-knit family and takes great pride and pleasure in nurturing her close relationships with her beloved nieces and nephews.

Please Review

Dear Reader,

If you enjoyed this book, would you kindly post a short review on Amazon? Your feedback will make all the difference to getting the word out about this book.

To leave a review, go to Amazon and type in the book title. When you have found it and go to the book page, please scroll to the bottom of the page to where it says 'Write a Review' and then submit your review.

Thank you in advance.